# Expecting the Unexpected

*A Collection of Stories by*

**B. B. Riefner**

Also by B. B. Riefner


*Mind Travels*
*A Child Too Near*
*Satan a Dog's Story*
*The Mad, Mad Magical Misery Tour*
*Reality Bytes.*
*The Teacher's Mind Travels*

Cover art: *The Last Man*, by Jack Hammond
Author photo by Marilyn Zucker

ISBN: 979-8-9992568-2-9

**Sligo Creek Publishing**
9039 Sligo Creek Parkway
Silver Spring, Maryland
https://www.sligocreekpublishing.com/

# Contents


Truth in Nakedness ...................................................... 1

A Child Too Near........................................................ 14

Nightmare for Pilgrims .................................................. 24

Let's Have Another Cup Of Coffee ...................................... 34

For Lovers and Sluggers ................................................ 44

Nightmare of Black on White: A Trilogy ....................... 52

    Part One: Dissonance................................................ 52

    Part Two: Adagio................................................... 54

    Part Three: Intermezzo ....................................... 60

Satan ... A Dog's Story .................................................. 64

*As for me, I am tormented with an everlasting itch
for things remote. I love to sail forbidden seas,
and land on barbarous coasts…*

~ MELVILLE

# Truth in Nakedness

## *Shirley or Shorely*


Admiration … Fascination … Lust … Concentration … Infatuation … all applied and only partially described the emotions ordinary males experienced watching Shirley Bordellos emerge from an automobile. As Shirley, who pronounced it *Shorely* in her deeply-etched New Jersey accent, stepped forth, males, even a few females, became visually transfixed by her physical perfection.

At this instant Shirley was sliding her overly long and perfectly shaped leg out of Aunt Lillian's vintage 1953 Nash Healy Convertible. Street resisted the visual delight and let his eyes drift to the portly, middle-aged neighbor watering his extensive flower gardens. Norris gave a slight disapproving head shake when it was obvious the neighbor was *so l*ost in his observations. He wasn't only drowning his roses, he was also destroying their lovely blooms.

Even though fully clothed, Shirley emerged from her seat more naked than Botticelli's *Venus Rising*. The pale, grape purple dress looked as though it had been sprayed on. Her hair and four-inch spiked heels' hue matched the dress exactly.

Carefully, Street closed the door and waved to the gardener. "She's really something, ain't she?" he called.

Delighted when the fellow ducked his head and half turned to the drowning roses. The move reminded Street of a child caught committing a social taboo.

"But you think she's worth losing both your garden and happy home for?"

Now his back was facing Norris who grinned when Shirley asked him not to be so nasty. Undeterred, Street concluded chastising the man with,

"You don't stand a chance, Buster. She's well read and likes discussing politics and religion."

"Norrus, I neveh knew yuh got such ah nasty tongue on yuh."

Carefully he ignored the comeback about his tongue, closed the door and made a sweeping gesture to encompass their total surroundings.

"So here we are in The Hamptons, the old money enclave of Towson, Maryland, Shirley. By the way, the cozy French provincial cottage back there about fifty yards or so, with its sixteen rooms belongs to my dear Aunt Lillian. Until you began throwing that popcorn at me two weeks ago, she was my favorite female on the planet."

"It's ah real spiffy place. She must be really loaded, huh?"

A truthful answer demanded more information than Street had ever managed to accumulate. Aunt Lillian had been a part of his life since his birth 42 years ago. To this day he had never been able to ascertain just how a first grade school teacher for 43 years could afford to live in such an exclusive development. Then again, his aunt had always been part enigma and part icon for him. Aunt Lillian had always been his *Life Guide*.

*Go out there and fight him. Doesn't matter if you win. Just don't let him bully you.*

He couldn't have been more than five when that advice was stamped in his brain.

*When you're with a new bunch, you got to estimate where you stand. In a group of ten, are you first, fifth or last. Whatever one that is, you have to assume the duties and obligations that position requires.*

That was at twelve and his first football team, when he told her how worried he was about making first string. He ended up the star.

*You can be an artist and do something else to support your art. But you can't be something else and an artist. Art won't take a back seat.*

That came the day before he married. Aunt Lillian had hit the bulls-eye again.

*Street, do not wait to do something you really need to do. Life goes like that,* and she snapped her fingers.

When he offered that she surely hadn't waited since she was just back from an unaccompanied tour of England and celebrating her seventy-eighth birthday, she shook her head. *No! Not me, you. Don't wait. Life goes faster than that snap.*

Street was now completely convinced.

"Yuh tink she's gonna be pleased when she sees me and asks what my occupation is and I tell her I'm stripping at dah *Silver Slipper Show Bar* in D.C. for ah couple ah weeks?"

Her question made him hesitate about confronting Aunt Lillian with Shirley. So he suggested they start in her extensive back yard garden and gazebo.

As he led Shirley to the gazebo, he thought, *If you have one flaw dear Aunt, It's you still judge people by how they dress, the color of their skin and their language usage. A generational habit you can't divorce yourself from. "Well, she's ...* And then he smiled. Shirley didn't seem to notice.

"Hey. Watcha tinken Norrus?" Shirley intoned.

"How much I like you in a pair of pumps and nothing else. No," he lied, and tried again. "I was wondering why you picked me to throw popcorn at."

"Oh, dat's real sweet, and dah udder's real easy. I liked yuhr beard, and yurh clothes. Yuh was really different from all dah perverts. Yuh looked like youse was ah artist, ah musician, ah writer, or maybe even ah paintah."

"Really. That's very flattering. And why, may I ask, do you like those types?"

"Dar usually real good in dah sack, and I was feeling my oats just den."

"Agh, dat's real sweet of youse Shurly."

That brought a wide smile followed by her explosive laugh. She even gave him a quick peck before she attempted to continue her interrogation concerning his aunt. Not wanting to reveal his lack of knowledge, Street managed to deflect the conversation's direction.

"Yuh know Norrus, I tought youse was ah musician when I threw dah corn at yuh."

"I was, once long ago. Mostly jazz. Bee-Bo ...far out crap."

"Really? I'll bet youse was ah trumpet player weren't yuh?" Startled Street could only nod." How'd yuh play? Soft or loud?"

"What it took, but I like playing thin, wispy like."

"Yeah. I always say ah trumpet ain't meant for no battle field blare, yuh know? It should be ah whisper in yurh ear as it unzips yurh fly."

Once more he shook his head, not able to restrain a smile of total admiration and awe at her strange ESP talents.

"So Shirley, you claim most of the arty types are good in the sack, but are there other reasons for your attraction to them?"

"Most of dem arh loonies but gentlemen. I've never met ah single one who liked going round smacking us gals. But I guess dah real reason is dah magic dey carry around with em."

"Hmm? Magic? You really mean it don't you?"

"Shur. Making music up in dah head or drawing us better den we look in ah mirrah is magic…and writers… ain't that what yuh do?"

She waited for him to acknowledge that fact.

"Youse guys are dah wildest, cause yuh can make ah movie screen out of ah page. Make word pitchers so real, we tink we can see and hear what's going on. Now dat's magic!" she exclaimed and gave him a triumphal smile.

"How's your magic?"

"No lamp to rub. I thought I could be something else and an artist. Turns out you can be an artist and something else as long as your art comes first. So, I gave up my first art…music… to get married and all the stuff.

"About fifteen years later I got up one morning and art was sitting on the edge of the bed and she kicked me right in the jaw when I climbed out. Been kicking me ever since…broke up my marriage. That still wasn't payment enough. Not for art. I'm convinced she's just gonna kick me in the teeth every day for the rest of my life."

"Can't yuh just kick her out? I did."

"You've got a few more years before the magic fifteen comes up. So be careful." He didn't like the gnawing down deep in his throat so he switched tracks.

"A lady once told me that the only two things a woman can't resist, are …

"Art and drive," she interrupted. Art mean being alive…Full of it."

"Exactly. She defined it as talent and vitality."

Shirley chose the long backed-bench in the Gazebo. She sat, leaned back and every lark and dove for a hundred yards sounded their delights.

"What stupid broad told yuh dis? She's gotta be nuts giving out trade secrets."

"And you've always managed to capture some of their art or drive, Shirley?"

"Surh. Most of youse ain't gotta selfish bone in yurh bodies, except when it comes to some parts of us or yurh art. It's ain't normal, yuh know? When dah art hits dah flesh, art wins hands down."

"So you've got it all carefully arranged. How come?"

Before she could offer either a lie or a confession, Norris added, "Just a second here … I'll bet the barn you wanted to be an artist, right?"

"A dansur. Ballet, and don't laugh! I loved it. But by dah time I was fourteen I got tired of all my straight partners copping ah feel, and most of dah fathers giving me dah eye, too. Besides,, my teacher told me dat I was just too big to be lifted by den, damn it."

"Wonders never cease." Street leaned against the railing. She didn't seem to notice the sarcasm hovering on the edges of his words.

"Yeah. Well, now I'm a strippah, which ain't too shoddy, yuh know? Cear about three grand ah week … Dat's tax free. And, I pick and choose who I do and who I dont."

"I am flattered."

"Is dat because I'm raping your head, or because yuh my *do*…yuh know?"

Her laugh almost aroused the ceramic geese nesting beside the slightly algae-tinted fish pond.

Now she began to survey his aunt's domain, and to take it all in, her torso shifted and rotated, so Street hardly heard a word.

"Dis is really ah nice place," Shirley chirped. "Yours is nice once yuh get inside, but yuh got too many damn books."

Street smiled as he recalled taking her to his house in Catonsville. It had been unoccupied since he took off almost two years ago. The memories, both tender and flesh-tearing almost erased her walking past him as he was entering. Aunt Lillian had sent her housekeeper … in to dust things when she was sure he was coming back to see his Mother.

As soon as she stepped into the living room, her eyes fastened on the twenty-four-foot long, floor to wall book case covering one entire wall. She walked over, ran a hand along a few bindings, snapped her wad of gum, and asked, "Jesus, yuh read all dese books, Narrus?"

When Street nodded and she let go a really loud laugh.

"Jesus Christ, when do yuh got time for udder stuff?" She moved back toward him, "Like me?"

She moved back towards him. "If I take off my dust jacket I'll bet yuh'll like m as much as yurh favorite book."

Later they were on the overstuffed and over-aged sofa. Her long legs draped over his thighs. "Well, you believe me now Narrus? Two times up to dah plate and yuh got a hit both of em. I don't trow popcorn at a guy unless I'm shur dey got enuff steam stored up for ah double header."

All he could do was grin and nod.

Exhaustion still couldn't dampen the sexual aura of a naked Shirley. So Street was taken aback, when she shifted to a whole new universe.

"Hey, can I borrow some of yuhr books for ah while?"

That shattered his image of her naked contentment. Her request shocked him so much he agreed instantly. He was even more shocked by that, since he made it a hard- kept rule to never lend his books…period. Slowly the ceramic birds came back into focus.

Slowly the ceramic birds came back into focus.

"Hey! Where yuh been? And when yuh gonna give me some of yuhr books? Or was dat a bunch of crap?"

"Not at all. And I was just thinking about the sofa and you, Shirley. And about the books … maybe some Hemingway?"

"Already read him."

Taking a breath to conceal his shock at her reply, he asked, "Oh? What have you read?@

"Dah Spanish Civil War ting … and dah one about dah guy who's impudent."

"Impotent … Jake Barnes is not brazenly immodest, Shirley, he's incapable of an erection."

"Yeah I felt sorry for him until he fell in love wit dah noble broad. I mean how can yuh fall in love when yuh can't get it up, Narrus? Dat ain't fair to us gals, yuh know?"

"Anything else?"

"Yeah. Dah one where dah guy who makes love to his chick after she's dead … Dah farewell ting."

She paused, and after deciding she was on the correct path and also that she had the right to tread this path, continued. "And yuh know what? Dis guy, Hemingway don't know dick about women."

"Really? Why do you say this?"

"He don't know squat about our cycle, Narrus."

"Do you mean the part in the book when he says she has to go, because she's knocked up?"

"Yeah … She's just had her period so it's no go. And if he don't know nuffin about dat, den he dont' know nuffin about us. He's edder a jerk or gay."

She stared at the books…shrugged and added, "Since he don't know nutting about us, is dat why he got married?

It took four or five inhalations, and a valiant effort to choke back a roaring laugh before Street he had better avoid this avenue.

"His short stories are better."

'Den Dey ain't about women, are Dey?"

Street could not suppress the smile. Even though it was not possible, somehow her ensemble didn't seem so.

"Okay, I surrender. How about if I lend you some Faulkner? You read him too?"

"I don't tink so. Ah drummer I knew said he's real hard. I need some entertainment. I got enuff bullshit going on in my life."

"Okay again. Some of his stuff is fairly easy. I'll loan you two easy and one hard one. How's that?"

"Sounds okay, I guess. I gotta trust youse. You've read dem, right?"

Street nodded, still astonished by the sudden change of direction. Then a bit of guilt crept in and to offset it he offered.

"My Aunt bought this place before the war. She's always been an emancipated lady. Could be she's one of the originals.

She bought her first car in 1920. It was a Ford, and she always claimed jumped bridges and aimed itself at stray cats.

"As early as I can remember, every summer, the day after school closed, she'd toss her bags in the back of some kind of car and take off alone. And she never came back until the day before she was due at school. She sent me lots of post cards."

"Yuh keep lots of em didn"t yuh?"

"Yes. How'd you guess?"

"Easy. You love dah lady. And when am I gonna meet yurh ideal broad?"

"Stay here and I'll get her. Nice day for tea in the garden."

As he rose, Street noticed the man watering his lawn had moved one house down where he and a less obese male could survey Shirley.

Street went to the car, got a pen and sheet of paper from the glove compartment then moved out of Shirley's view. He stopped before he began imitating his Aunt's broad, *Seven Sister's* style to view the three well-dressed ladies across the low hedge. He knew exactly who they were watching and exactly what they were saying about her.

He imagined his aunt's reactions as he composed.

Her glasses are on the very end of her aristocratic nose, as she measures Shorely's in three separate stages, starting with the shortness of her skirt and ending with the grape curls. When Shirley can't hear them anymore, she'll say, *I hope you told her she can't use the bathrooms?*

The last one would be as Shorely trooped down the path to his car while he stayed to kiss his aunt goodbye.

*Thank the Lord you're getting her out of here before house prices fall any further than she's already caused, Street.*

And just about then Aunt Lillian would finally throw the sink at him.

*When will you grow up? Don't you think that it's about time you gave up being a teenager still trying to shock your elders?*

Street finished the note, and as he slowly counted to a hundred, decided as soon as he could he would call Aunt Lillian and tell her answer to that last one. Before he went back to *Shorely,* he carefully turned and waved at the women still gathered on the side lawn across the street. He was pleased that at least they didn't turn away, even though they made it quite obvious they were ignoring his antics.

At one hundred he turned and went back to Shirley, waving the note as soon as he was in her line of sight. "Hey! Aunt Grace is at the hospital visiting a dear friend, the one who gave her the ceramic geese over there. She left a note on the hall table."

"Really?"

"Says she's looking forward to meeting you. She even wants us to come to dinner." When he saw her suspicions, he handed her the note. "Here," and her doubts disappeared instantly.

Shirley and he spent the rest of a nice Sunday evening at his home. The meal he prepared amazed her.

"Ah never met ah guy who could cook dis good Narus. Yuh hadda had a really smart broad help yuh learn how to cook dis good. And what the hell is dis?"

"It's a very old French fisherman's dish. Whatever they didn't sell that day went into the pot that evening. Lots of the really expensive dishes started out in peasant's kitchens. I got a book on that too. You want to borrow it?"

"Ain't got no time for cooking. It ain't got any squid or octopus in has it?"

He lied. She ate two full helpings.

"Do you like poetry? he asked as he began picking out some works.

"Poets are mostly gay ain't dey? I ain't in tuh faggots."

"Did you know that a poet named E.E. Cummings was a bouncer in a Paris whorehouse after the First World War?"

"Suhr. Didn't yuh know dat all dah bouncers in Paris whore houses were poets?"

Street stopped searching and waited a few seconds before he turned.

"You sure of that?"

"How dah hell should I know. I ain't ever been to Paris, Narrus!" and she fell onto the sofa she was laughing so hard. Street stared for a couple seconds and then laughed almost as hard.

"Touché. I deserved that."

"Yeah. I ain't even gotta high school education, but dat wasnt fair, yuh know?"

He nodded and went back to harvesting some Faulkner. Her shot made him add two works he hadn't thought would be suitable until now.

Late that night he dropped her off at her hotel just over the Potomac River, in Virginia. As she dismounted she held Faulkner's <u>Fifty Stories</u>, plus the novels <u>Sanctuary</u> and <u>Light in August.</u>

Eight A.M, the next morning, his phone rang.

"Hi Narrus."

"What do you want at this ungodly hour?"

"Two tings. First off I read two of dem stories. I didnt hit dah sack till three. And ah nuddeer ting! Dis guy is really ah sick cookie."

"He also won the *Nobel Prize*, Shirley. You can't tear a *Nobel* winner to bits."

"Prize … smize!" There was a pause. "Narus, don't try to screw up mah head. But do people really sleep wit dead bodies? And if dey do, is it Southern Hill-Billy's only? I mean dis broad had dat guy in her bed for…Jesus."

"Not usually but occasionally, and the South has no monopoly."

"Okay, but for forty or fifty years? I was scared out of my mind when I got to dah part about the single piece of iron gray hair in dah bed with dah guy's skeleton."

"What's the second?"

"Story or reason?"

"Story first."

"Dah one about dah bear. I didn't understand it, but I really liked it. It's ah hunt. So why don't dah kid shoot? As I said, it's too complicated."

"Good. I'm not amazed at either of your answers. What's your other reason?"

"My agent's got me booked for Miami tomorrow night."

"Oh?" He tried not to let his disappointment creep in. "Thought you said we had a full month?"

"Yeah …Me too…But dat's ah long time for perverts to stay interested in one body, yuh know? Even when it's as good as mine."

"Gottcha."

"I was wondering if it's okay if I keep dah books and mail em to yuh later?"

"Sure ... by the way, <u>The Bear</u> is about *Rites of Passage* ... the price a boy has to pay to become a man."

"Dat's spelled r-i-t-e ... right? I'll read it again."

"Do that."

"Wanna get together? I can book ah flight as late as 10 tonight?"

"You trying to pay me back for the books?"

"No, you jerk. You're ah really nice guy. And we made it work ... didn't we?"

There was a long pause and then she added, "I wish I got to meet yuhr aunt though."

"Me too ... and what about lunch? I can pick you up about noon and take you to the airport?"

Suddenly ... Street knew this was all wrong.

"About my Aunt, Shirley...she wasn't at a hospital...she always takes a nap that time of day."

He took a deep breath and swallowed ... "I wrote the damned note I told you she had written. I'm so ... I didn't want her to ... I just took you out there to give her a little jolt. And I ... Jesus...Aunt Lillian is always asking me when I'm going to grow up and I usually say ..."

"Neveh! Right? But dis time yuh knew dis wasn't ah good ting to do, right?"

"I'll be damned. You saw right through ..."

"Of course! I knew dat, you dope. What do youh take me for?"

"A really intelligent person I treated like ..."

"A lady, Narrus. Don't beat your-self too hard, hear me? You did a sweet ting writing dat note. Even if you're too embarrassed to see it right now."

"Would you still like to do lunch with me?"

"Of course your big boob. But how about making it one? I gotta pack if you're gonna take me."

Before Street could tell her how happy he was she didn't hate him she added, "And Narrus ... meet me in my room, Okay?"

She had a flight out of Baltimore's Martin Luther King Airport, so they had to leave sooner than he wanted. Once she piled all four suitcases behind his seat in the tiny trunk, she stepped in without bothering to open the door.

"Always liked convertibles when dah top is down. Gives me ah big advantage, do it?" He laughed and nodded.

Street drew into the curb and unloaded her luggage and motioned at the trio of Red Caps charging her way. "Those guys know a good tipper when they see one," he grinned.

"I isn't gonna see yuh any more, aint I?"

"I'll be in Mexico. I'll find a beach. You'll love it. Lots of sun and ... I'll write and you could come on down. I know?"

Her rueful smile dismissed that fantasy. She stepped closer. "I'll read dah stuff and send it to you before youse cut out.@

Street reached out, pulled her to him, careful to keep the lower parts of him at a respectful distance, but nosing her coned hair. "Look," he almost whispered into its slight stiffness, "keep 'em. Read everything."

"I will ... Promise." She stepped free and turned to the winning Red Cap, and motioned at her luggage. Then she came back to him.

"Narrus dat's dah nicest ting any man's given me in ah long, long time. I'll take real good care of em, promise"

"I Know. And I wish ..."

"Yeah, me too, and I ain't wished dat in ah long, long time."

She stepped back, blew him a kiss, and then turned to follow her luggage. But she had to add, "Remember! Popcorn's ah great pick up. So long."

Now she did walk away and Street watched, and thought that the gawking, twisting male wake she caused reminded him the way the really big waves broke... hard... heavy... and deadly ... unless you were experienced or desperate enough to deal with them.

Aunt Lillian's message blinked at him when he entered his study. She picked up the first ring.

"Hi. It's your favorite nephew."

"Are you still with some half-naked floozy? When are you going to grow up?"

"It was...look, I did, darling Aunt. Her name's Shirley and she did it. And at first it hurt like hell. But now..."

"It always does. Well, I'm sorry I didn't meet her. Must be something if she's made you grow up."

"She is as bright, as independent and tough as you."

Aunt Lillian sighed and asked when he was taking her to lunch. They talked for a few more minutes, as both his and her words dissolved before they reached his ears, and Shirley's last smile perched right on his desk top.

He decided to rent his home. That took two more weeks, and another one to get Aunt Lillian settled in her own retirement community. As he had his last lunch with her and was walking to his car, he turned and stared at the impressive front of the *Masonic Home for Ladies*.

*You gals just don't have a clue, do you? You've just had the Grande Dame come aboard and things will never be the same again until she's no longer a passenger,* he declared to the walls. But that wasn't his concern.

He decided he needed some respite and *The Pie* possessed too dramatic and image to resist.

# A Child Too Near

The first time Kurt Wachter drove into Northern Mexico he expected Mariucci bands attired in huge sombreros and bejeweled jackets. However, once he cleared border customs, drove a totally dessert, unpaved, blacked out street and passed the last bent street light, it was hours before he saw traces of another living soul. The emptiness went on mile after mile; the edges of the poorly paved, single lane asphalt road were a continuous ash dump. Its contamination so lush it only permitted an occasional clump of drooping weeds. The countryside's complexion resembled an old, unshaven man.

Then suddenly, in what seemed the most inhospitable area of the Sonora Desert, groups of women and children began appearing beside the two lane almost empty road. Just like the struggling colonies of weeds and grasses, they sat in scattered bunches. They were totally female but of varying ages, with complexions exactly the same as the piles of fading abandoned plastic bags.

The first group surprised him but after he passed two or three more, he started wondering where they lived. Even this shallow interest level started him searching the screen of cactus and dry brush which began appearing just before he spied the first bunch. There were no ruined buildings, but now, suddenly, there were women and children on both sides of the road. 'The ruined living on top of ruins,' Kurt thought. His second silent question followed instantly. 'Why are they out here in this heat?'

Wachter half decided that perhaps they were all waiting for buses or trucks to take them to towns. It had been at least two full hours since he sped through a cluster of totally dark, sagging adobe single story buildings. There had been only a few dirt tracks joining the sticky black ribbon in almost that same length of time since he had passed through what resembled a settlement. Even the dirt tracks had shown little signs of recent traffic.

For over half an hour he passed group after group, traveling at a steady fifty-five miles an hour. Ethnocentric fears and general ignorance prevented him from stopping. Kurt could not imagine doing that, even if he stayed in his magic chariot and let them come to him.

That was when he began to notice there were small shelters made from twigs and dead limbs. They were back off the road. Some were almost out of view. Most had no roofs but the ones that did were covered with torn and faded plastic sheets; plastic, which seemed to him a fragile shield from the fierce and uncompromising heat.

He also soon realized each group simply sat among the weeds or tallest cactus. But the instant they saw his car, a child, always the smallest and always a girl, raced to the edge of the road waving a small box or cage, skipping back and forth.

Wachter always increased his speed whenever one of them ran toward him, until he realized he was going more than eighty miles an hour. It seemed totally unreasonable that he could travel that fast, still keep the car on the uneven road, and at the same time take in so much detail. For a time he thought they were just another mirage, the same as the retreating lakes he drove toward with relentless determination. However, the women and children did not vanish as he reached them, or taunt him by appearing well in advance and running for an instant just ahead of his hood ornament. Then he passed a single child standing too near the road.

"Jesus Christ! She'll get sucked right into the slip-stream!" he shouted into his windshield. As the car roared by, her frail reflection instantly appeared in his rear view mirror. She was rocking slightly, but she was safe. Then Kurt saw her fall to the asphalt surface, and even though that image disappeared from his viewing area, he did not slow down.

Half an hour later, once he was assured the male was an American, he picked up a hitch hiker, whose clean, neat appearance bore him no threat. The hitch hiker declared he wasn't going far, could not drive, but he did speak in perfect Californian when asked about the people by the road.

"Selling birds, dude. Got little birds in those cages. Trying to get you to stop and buy 'em." After smiling at Wachter's surprise, he asked, "Hey man, got any cigarettes? Could really go for a smoke right now ... been dry almost all day, prince ... a real drag."

Annoyed by the hitch hiker's request to contaminate his car, and not bothering to introduce himself, Kurt decided to be just as aloof. "So where are they getting all these birds from?" He used his best classroom come-to-order tone.

"They catch 'em in the desert. Gotta spend a day or so making them little cages, I guess. The women do all that. Not sure though. But you'll never see anyone but women on the road. They get their kids to try and sell 'em to us Gringos as we zoom past." Then he opened his mouth and a huge "*ZOOOOOOM!*" came forth, blotting out the noise of the overworked air conditioner.

"But what can anyone do with them? Getting a bird through customs is tougher than getting drugs over the border."

"I'm not too hip on why, prince. Some Mexican once told me you earn good luck when you set 'em free. The Dude, as Wachter silently labeled him, stared off into the mirages for a couple of breaths, and then concluded, "Maybe that's a little far-fetched."

"Not if it's an ancient tradition."

"Tradition ... sedition ... who cares?" The Dude tossed his head, frowned, then added, "Could be you could get extra credit from God for showing mercy ... I guess."

"Or it could be an offering to their gods," Kurt mused, ignoring the obvious sarcasm.

"Yeah, could be that. But you know the more you think about it, it's just probably a way to earn some extra money. May be the only way they have for staying alive out here, you know?"

"No, I don't, but you're probably right. There's sure as hell nothing out here. You can't grow food in dust and rocks."

"Maybe they are just selling 'em so you can open the cage and set them free."

"Jesus, that's really stupid." He was not sure the man was telling the truth, but he was certain The Dude was enjoying his superiority regarding the local customs.

"By the way, I didn't get your name."

"Harry King." The accompanying large smile convinced Kurt he was lying. Finding the cultural differences too stark, Wachter' blood pressure eased when "The Dude" told him that he was getting out at the next paved cross road, and lapse into silence then dozed off.

It was over an hour before he reached the cross roads King had indicated as his destination. It was completely devoid of any signs of human habitation. The four roads vanished into the horizon, and there were no sign posts. As he halted, the passenger woke from his nap.

"Hey, thanks! You're a prince. Just wish you had a smoke. That would make it perfect, man." As he said this, he reached into the back seat and retrieved his heavy, dust encrusted leather pack, before he stepped gingerly over the melting asphalt to the dusty apron.

He was about to turn away when his features and stance shifted into a semi-serious mode as he offered, "Hey man, there's a really nice village about two hundred clicks down this road," and he pointed to the one leading west.

"Right by the Pacific man ... it's unspoiled. Want to give it a go?" Wachter's silence urged a bit more of his sales pitch, as he shouldered his load.

"Great place to lie back and let the world go by. Always some great looking half naked Dutch and totally naked German chicks, you know?"

The invitation was turned down as Kurt's stark visual projections centered on being murdered and all his belongings sold so that four or five unkempt Americans could enjoy a few more days of sloth.

"Pemex station's about fifteen more clicks, and then there's absolutely nothing for another three maybe four hours, till you get out of this. Rest of the way after that's real pretty." There was a long pause while The Dude waited for some sort of reply. Finally he added, "First time into Mexico?"

"Been over the border, but this is the first time I've been this far south."

"They're nice people. It's really a beautiful country and you gotta admire the way they can all make do with little or nothing." Then with a nod, Harry turned and sat down by the road and dismissed him.

It was almost twice as far as Harry King claimed. The Pemex gasoline station was attached to a filthy looking restaurant, advertising air conditioning. So after getting a fill up, he decided to go in. Later he often wondered if that act was the greatest mistake of his life up to that point. ... Or a mile stone of random wisdom.

Two Americans sat at a table in the very center of the nearly empty room. Their postures resembled terrified survivors at Custer's Last Stand. After he finished buying a cold draft beer, they motioned for him to join them. He quickly discovered they were not really Americans.

"Just a couple of retired adventurous Californians from L.A. Gotta admit this would make one hell of a place for a senior prom, right?"

The man rose and held out his hand as he added. "This is my wife, Irene, and I'm Alex." He was tall, tanned and instantly claimed that they were bored.

For the next ten sentences or so Kurt carefully agreed with them about Mexico's desperation, its heat, the bad roads, and their terribly dangerous truck drivers.

"How about those people back there with the birds? What are they up too?" After he told them what King offered Alex nodded wisely.

"So they really are selling the birds!" Alex announced as he and his wife exchanged knowing glances.

"Poor little things," Irene offered between sips of beer straight out of the old fashion brown glass bottle. "They got nothing, I can see." Irene had a very pointy nose. Salesmen had always told Kurt that people with pointy noses were generally difficult sells.

"I didn't want Lex to stop. But he's so hard headed. One day we'll be in it up to our necks and he'll learn to listen."

"One little kid who looked like she was gonna die from starvation, ran up and started yammering. Sounded like a little dog. If they want to sell us something they should learn some English. You agree?"

Kurt started a negative answer, but it was instantly erased.

"Neither of us had a clue," Irene protested.

"So you're saying that maybe all she wanted was for me to buy a bird?"

"For all we knew they could just be trying to get us out of the car to rob us."

Alex frowned, then waved to the sole waiter mopping the floor with dirty water and a mop that had half of its strings missing. When he got some attention, Alex motioned for three more beers.

"I didn't want her bird. Might have if I knew what it was for. Thing was damn near dead as far as I could see. Didn't want her touching me either."

"The guy I picked up was pretty sure she was trying to sell it so you could let it go. "

"Buy a bird in a box and let it go? Even Lex isn't fool enough to do that."

"Jesus, a whole bunch of them came running that one time we did stop ...too many for me. Besides, Irene was screaming her fanny off to get out of there so I buzzed off, pronto."

Alex paid for the three new beers and took a deep swallow. "I'm surprised. But you gotta admit, they really got good beer down here, you know?"

It was obvious to him that Alex was just getting warmed up, but Kurt had, had enough. He left his beer untouched and excused himself. Back in the heat, before he could cool the interior down again, he was never able to explain why he turned back.

As the drive back began, he realized it had been a really long distance since he had seen the bird people. It was going to be endless hours before he got back to the child. So Kurt constructed his own vision of the little girl's life to pass the time and ignore the lack of scenery.

When he arrived, she would be just this side of starvation; an orphan thrown out of her village. Even the lowest of the village poor ignored her. It took her two days filled with desperation to find a bird. She finally stole one in another's trap before anyone saw her. All the rest of that day she worked on a crude cage. While she made it, she kept the bird tied by one foot to a tiny bush, until it was too tired to even struggle. That reminded her of the state she was in right then.

When she got to the road, she was very happy because now she had the means for acquiring food. Her teeth were almost worn flat from sucking on tiny pebbles. She sold this bird, and taught herself how to catch more. When she got very good there were many birds in beautiful cages, and all of them were sold. In time she bought many pretty clothes.

In a few years she got successful enough that she hired old people to make cages for her. She bought a little shack, but later became rich enough to buy a new house. After that she let all the old, poor people live in her shack if they wanted. Now the whole village loved and respected her, and she helped everyone in need. He decided that even included those who had been the cruelest to her.

After several hours, he began looking for vendors. When none appeared, Kurt pushed the car through the descending darkness, no longer trying to erase the tangled similarities between the dead brush, the barren sand, screeching incarcerated birds, stoic Indian women, heaps of discarded trash, and the child he saw keel over through his rear view mirror. Desperate for all of it to dissolve, another scenario was concocted.

It takes her two days to reach the road after stealing the bird. She nearly freezes through the long sleepless nights, and when she arrives the other women force her to move far down the road. They jeer when she tries to explain how desperate she is. They call her a fool, and ask if she thinks they were all rich. They mock her unmercifully until she moves away.

She carries her sickly bird in the crude twig cage past the groups of squatting children and women. The young girls call out terrible insults. They laugh and ask, 'And how can you expect to sell a dying bird to the Gringos?'

A woman sneers and tells her all the Gringos will do is spit on her as they pass. A small, dirty boy walks beside her and shouts that the Gringos will stop … take her bird … not pay for it … and run over it as they leave.

She sits far away from the others watching as the heat slowly tries to fry the road, and there are only a few cars. None of them slow down. As they fly by, their slip stream pulls at her ragged dress.

Then there is the waiting day after day without a single car stopping near her. Those who do are always too far up the road for her to reach before they drive off. Once she manages to draw close enough to yell out her price, but two children and a woman throw rocks at her. Although none of them hit her, she feels like a village cur.

Each night she sleeps in a ditch. Her water bottle is empty, and every night she almost freezes because the air comes down from the nearby mountains.

Her lips become painfully cracked. Once the sun is high, the heat tries to pull the hair from her head by its roots. Her toes swell and her feet sting from her journey. She pleads with the women for water. They refuse for one full day, but when she awakens, there is a full can of it by her head. Also some worm carved bread.

For a short time, on the fifth day, there is a line of cars. Some pull over before speeding off like angry monsters flying across the hot, rough blackness of the road. One comes toward her, and as it flies by, it tears at her clothes and hair, as if trying to steal her only possessions. She is suddenly shaken to her senses by a gringo.

Wachter tries vainly keeping Alex and Irene's faces blurred. Irene waits a few feet behind her husband, using his bulk to ward off any diseases the child possesses. Instantly the child holds up her bird, praying it still lives. Sensing its only hope for life has arrived, it chirps and jumps about the cage.

The child smiles her best urchin's smile. Her eyes implore the Gringos to buy. In short sentences she explains her plight. Holding back nothing, and forgetting all her pride, she tells them she no longer feels pain. She says the old women of her village claim you are dying when you know the pain is there but cannot feel it. She says it is the most dangerous sign of starvation. She tells them she is seeing beans and tortillas all about their faces.

They look at her blankly. Irene wants to leave at once. She is positive the child is infected with things she has never dreamt of. All the time, she yells, questioning why he stopped in the first place. She denounces him for bringing her to Mexico rather than Las Vegas. She screams that saving money isn't any fun when she's terrified all the time. Her complaints are endless.

Alex tells her he thinks the child is trying to sell them the bird. Irene screams louder for them to leave. Alex holds up two fingers and grins his best Chamber of Commerce smile. She yells at him for offering two dollars for the mangy bird, and whines for him to get back in their car. He pretends to exam the bird. By now great wet stains form a pious collar about her neck and bandoliers across his chest.

Alex assures Irene he is only offering two hundred pesos, just about sixteen cents. Then he turns to the child and says this is his final offer. He's determined not to be the one who spoils these people with high prices. The child is bewildered and stands with the cage thrust forward, her mouth open, while Alex swears he cannot believe anyone can be so stupid. 'How can you bargain when you don't know any English,' he mocks.

Frustrated, he turns and starts toward their car. Irene rushes to catch up, smiling at the thought of getting back into the air-conditioning. He starts the engine as the child runs around to his side of the car. Her legs are too weak and she collapses before she can call out. For a tantalizing minute he seems about to get out to investigate. Then he eases the car onto the road and drives off. The unconscious child does not see or hear the two large coins he drops on the road.

Wachter concludes constructing his mental movie with the child laying face up, dying as the greedy sun eats her brain. After she is dead, the tiny yellow bird works frantically, trying to enlarge the small split caused by the cage falling on its edge. Finally it frees itself, but is too weak and mutilated to fly. It hops into the nearest bush and waits for an ant to pass by.

Just before dusk Kurt reaches the first group of women. He is unsure of the child's location, so he leans out and yells slowly and loudly in English, at two women staring at him from under the shelter of a large leafless bush. "The little girl. The one alone. Where is she?"

The women both laugh and point at him. The oldest one lifts a cage with a yellow bird screaming for its freedom. Kurt refuses to leave the car, certain that as long as he stays in it he is invincible. He silently swears that when he finds her he will take her back across the border, place her in a good school, and pay for all her expenses. He almost believes she is really an orphan.

He drives up the apron, carefully looking in the shallow ditch and also into each shelter. He tries to recall what she looks like. When Wachter does not locate her, he turns and retraces his route. The sun is sliding behind the faintly purple mountains. This is the signal for the women to begin gathering up their cages and children. After they have all disappeared, he gets out and begins searching the edges of the desert. This seems to him that he is lifting the edges of a carpet looking for one tiny lost item, but this carpet is a thousand square miles. Then, it's suddenly too dark to see the edges of the road only a few yards away. He is caught in a blackness which mocks the concept of direction.

He turns and stumbles through the brush until the road and his car are back in view, and he is relieved to find it hasn't been vandalized. Wachter visualizes invisible scores of dangerously desperate men are all around him and he thinks he hears machetes scraping against the rocks and bushes.

He jumps in the car, and locks the doors before starting its engine. It roars in the dark like some wounded beast. Its tires dig in. Then the back swings around, sways and weaves until they find traction, and flee along the thread of head lights. Somehow he believes that his efforts have emancipated his concerns. That he is once again free and back in control.

The car cares nothing about the secrets contained along the edges of the road. Its lights reveal only instants of this alien world as they push the curtains of darkness aside. It is minutes before he admits this is not another plot line.

Kurt curses Wachter for making such a stupid effort. Then he gradually slips into a more optimistic mood which enables him to convince his guilt she is safe.

More than likely she is in her house right now, eating some beans and laughing about him and all the other crazy Gringos with her parents. He decides they have sold many birds that day. Tomorrow they can take the day off and go to the market. Her mother says she can have the dress she likes so. It's the third new dress this month.

Then that evaporates along with the wet edges on his windshield. "No! None of that is worth a dime! When the hell are you gonna see that the only way to get out of this cosmic joke we call living is to stop by the side of life's roadways, every time you see someone who looks like they need help? No matter how dangerous it is. No matter how! Oh hell! Just do it! Don't drive by someone falling on their face!"

The endless impenetrable black edging the road mocks his oath.

# Nightmare for Pilgrims

Once again Street Norris was the lonesome traveler. Rome's Saint Peter's Square was lightly occupied, even almost empty; at least as empty as that famous square can ever be imagined. Most of the Summer Catholics from the U.S. were gone. Along with them went his current mate, who was responsible for almost three full months of erotic intoxications.

He decided to ignore entering the Basilica or spend six dollars to roam through the city of museums. Instead, he opted to sit the remainder of the day away somewhere in the square. He was thinking about his last conversation with Cindy Dillon.

"The world is mad, you know?" She said it in her most cynical mode. "This place either demands you seek sainthood or cynicism. What made you take the easy path, Bear?"

"I met too many true believers who claim the only way you can get to God is to go up."

Norris smiled, almost ready to agree, but wanting their last words, his last look at her freshness and vitality, to last just a few minutes more.

"Old. Emmanuel Kant says take any method in order to reach your madness."

"That's you. You like the two married ... religion and madness."

"Well, at least religion and superstitions. They are matching hand maidens."

"That's just the glib side of you. We've been looking at this shrine and that shrine all summer. You remind me of a birddog quartering a field. You're the one looking for The Mystical Revelation."

"My daughter claims I will only accept it if I am struck down like Paul on my way to where ever."

Cindy was about to depart for America to complete her Masters in Italian Economic History, and Street Norris was annoyed he had not been able to convince her to skip her fall term and join him in Turkey.

"Anyway, you got to admit the only thing they all had in common was we had to go up to reach God or His buddies, which is unadulterated crap. If you want to get to God, you got to reach out, Norris. Even that kid who lived next door, Mickey S. De Angelo knew that."

He now admitted that she had been right, for he was already missing her flesh, desperately. He wished she were here so he could tell her that the real, least common denominator was God appeals to none unless they were barefoot.

Reflecting, trying to keep her scents about him, he also decided that their final day had been either a disaster, if he looked at it from a sexual prospective, or a tragedy, if he took a romantic view.

*She wanted the only commodity I am always short on ... affection, rather than my strength ... passion*, he concluded as he mentally redesigned the summer's events to meet his mood.

He did not see the two well-dressed and attractive young women, until they were almost upon his position, beneath one of the huge columns on the shady west side of the square. Street sensed a whiff of destiny when the taller of the two asked in beautiful Spanish if he spoke English. His immediate reaction was to address the lesser of the two beauties, even though it was the latter who had spoken. She appeared to be the elder, and Norris, who considered himself an excellent judge of a beautiful women answered that it was the only language he really could speak. It was one of his pet theories, that beautiful women were too interested in their own beauty until they were twenty-five. He was convinced that it took that long for them to accept mortality, and rid themselves of the need for a pretty male's attention all the time. He decided after a careful though hasty inspection, both of this pair was still very interested in pretty as well as boys. Except their sighs of relief, as beautiful as their features, they raised not one iota of false hopes for the immediate future.

"Please come," the older one said.

"Of course, Senorita."

"Your services are needed at once!" the second one added. "And your Spanish is interesting ... a nice street flavor, senor." Then her tone did a complete turnabout. "There is a very sick woman on the far side of the square. We saw you and were almost positive you are an American. This poor woman refuses to speak to anyone in any language but English."

"We're sure she is English, though. She babbles just like them"

"She could be an American," Norris offered.

"Oh, impossible! She's dressed far too elegantly to be an American," the older one intoned. Norris seldom bothered to defend or attack his native land, so he followed them across the square.

They made the journey in utter silence, which allowed him to admire his potential catch more closely, and decided on the more mature one as his target. He was rehearsing his most intriguing line, when asked what his occupation was.

"*I have never had to work, my dear,*" and was already assured that his favor would garner him at least the opportunity for companionship. Perhaps the remainder of his stay would be even more interesting than his summer with Cindy.

As he followed them, his plans of occupation were interrupted by the memory one of his friends had once made about Italian women *Look at them. All they do is primp and preen. What will they do once their country becomes Communist? In Communism, all have to work.*' Norris never thought of telling Wanda, the Polish Baroness, that women like this would continue to *work* at the same trade they had pursued for the last seven-thousand years. He also didn't proclaim, *Italy will be commie when we eat the moon, Wanda.*

Once they arrived at the eastern side of the square, it only took one look for Norris to agree that he was confronting a very sick person. As he walked, he had had a mental picture of physical illness. Some poor woman was in the throes of vomiting. He was even more surprised when he turned to tell his guides he had no intentions of helping someone who was crazy, and they chirped "Ta ta" in unison and slipped away before he could answer.

*Ta, ta*, he thought. *Sounds like you really get a lot of practice with that poor soul.*

Then, he turned to the *Poor Soul.*

Her upper attire was immaculate. She wore a perfectly tailored tweed of the finest Shetland Wool. It was a light fawn, which Norris considered not only his favorite color, but also the acme of upper-class taste. The white shirtwaist was the perfect background for the small figured woolen necktie which had been the vogue about twenty-five years ago for academia. The *Harris Tweed* hat was a deeply rich brown, which matched the style if not the hue of her suit.

However, when he glanced at her legs, he confronted complete incongruities. Her light brown stockings were woolen, filled with holes and as filthy as a camel driver's cloak. For shoes she wore flaps of uncured leather, bent over her toes, and held in place by rawhide strips that went under her arch and were tied in a tangle of knots just below where her ankles merged with her feet. One piece of leather was soft side out, while the other was its opposite. The footwear reminded Street of a pair of gloves suitable for a giant. Of course he was fascinated because for Norris, there were only two types of persons who created such a state. Women who were strange, and showed little concern for conventions, and young ladies with the same qualities. As he appraised her, she was thumbing a very frayed and limp address book, and was extremely wrought. Her lips were twisted with terrible disappointment.

"Are you Okay? Can I help?" Norris would have liked to retract the *okay* for, *Anything wrong, Madame?* It seemed more fitting if he did not look below her waist. There was no mistaking the relief which instantly appeared with his first word.

"Oh, please! Have you got it?" She continued to flip the pages of her battered, leather covered book. Each time she got to its end, she held it out in one hand and carefully gave it a gentle shake. Street waited to see if whatever she was looking for would fall out.

"I had it right here, but I have misplaced it."

She shook it again, this time vigorously, as if she was punishing it. Suddenly her lips were twisted with a grimace of pain.

"I've had it right here, the entire time I traveled here! Kept it, right here, in the back with the other numbers! Now, when I am finally here and need it, it's gone! I do this all the time! I lose everything I own! It simply runs away from me and hides!"

She gave Street her first full look and then added, "How can I keep doing that?"

Each sentence increased in both volume and frustration. She didn't allow Street to say he lost his keys or eyeglasses at least twice each day. "Have you got it? I mean do you have it with you? It would be wonderful if you did!"

"What is it?"

Instantly, she became unfocused again, retreating to turning and returning the pages. He asked several times how he could help her, but she ignored him. He was about to leave when she suddenly refocused and stared directly into his eyes.

"Do you have it? Please tell me, you do. I need it so!"

"Maybe, but what is it?"

Instantly, she began shaking her head violently from side to side.

"NO! NO! NO!!! I told them I needed someone who had it with them! I told them I wouldn't speak to anyone unless they had it. So, they brought you! And so, do you have it? Yes or no? If you do, don't torture me! Give it here, please!"

Street slowly began to edge away as passers-by turned at her cries. A few were beginning to form a rough circle, and they seemed to have only one expression. They looked as though he was about to commit an act either illegal or immoral; perhaps both. She followed him this time with her feet as well as her eyes. He almost made the sign of the cross as she did.

"What is it you need?" He asked the question for the benefit of the onlookers who were drawing even nearer.

Immediately, she responded with, "Do you have it? Do you have the phone number?"

Right then he wanted to walk away even if he did confess he went out of his way to meet the mad of the earth. Madness was a trait he never wanted to ignore. But insanity was a state he shunned without hesitation. So he asked what number she wanted and when she looked puzzled, he got a bit sarcastic and asked if she needed the one for Saint Peters.

When she claimed to have that one, he asked, "Do you want the one for the Pope or just the one for Christ?"

He called it out loud enough for the gathered and glowering three rows of spectators to hear clearly. Their faces did not give one hint that he had managed to communicate. They all appeared to have sided with insanity. Street thought perhaps a

Mass for the insane had just exited, or perhaps the ten or so buses parked in two rows, had brought a full complement of the insane for the Papal Blessing. Suddenly, his concern to flee was overcome by one which cast him in the role of a cat stalking its next meal. It also felt like she was a mouse who had gladly waited for the cat to arrive.

"You want God's number, don't you? Is that what you want?" Of course, she nodded her head vigorously. Now, Norris only wanted to take leave of this mad woman. So, in a very condescending tone he said, "I must have left it back in my hotel. I promise, I'll get it and come right back."

The small mob started to melt into the backdrops. As he was leaving, she called out her heartfelt thanks. He retreated to the only place he was sure she would not follow him. Since he had always hated all religions, it was only reasonable to hate Catholicism the most and despise Saint Peters since that was its most conspicuous monument. He despised it for its size; he ridiculed its dedication to glorifying the things Christ preached against, led a revolt against, and died for. He often claimed, the tenets Christ advocated had lost. *Show me three people who have the same belief and I will show you intolerance in the name of either its god or mercy*, was one of his most pompous claims.

When a visitor enters Saint Peters, they are supposed to feel small, insignificant, unworthy, and sin-filled. The colonnades become the arms of the Church embracing, gathering in all sinners to forgive their sinning and save their souls. Street Norris always entered it with the feeling he was a giant, carrying tidings of doom. Any love he still managed to hoard for his fellow man vanished instantly. He advocated some well-placed-explosives were what was needed because ruined religious structures were much more attractive. To him the empty and ruined ones were absolutely fascinating.

He'd been inside many times. He was a world traveler who returned to old familiar places over and over again, and sometimes brought new companions to guide through whatever civilization he needed as a background for seduction. Norris was always interested to see how much more had been adopted, in order to maintain it competing in the ever shrinking world. He was convinced that sooner or later all the great places of antiquity would have the charm of international airports.

*At least then, we shall all feel perfectly at home and divested of fear and awe. We may even see that the need to be at them has vanished,* he pontificated as he led one willing ward after another through the mazes of various cultures.

Once he gained its safety, Norris decided to stroll about choosing to go counter-clock- wise, so he could watch the expressions of the devout or the bored. There was no difference actually, and besides, he often found delightfully attractive women in such places. Art galleries were the best hunting grounds, but churches occasionally held some success.

As he walked along the dark southern base of *The Barn*, he suddenly saw a phone booth tucked back in one of the darker niches. Since it was unlighted, it was easily mistaken for either a part of the wall or a confessional.

He became excited when the door responded to his hand's pressure. He saw immediately that it contained a phone. Once inside and the door closed, his eyes became adjusted to the dimness. There was no seat, which was annoying, but the antique phone quickly overcame his disappointment.

The phone was black. When he touched it, his thoughts leaped back forty or more years to his childhood, when a four number digit was followed by some letter, and a human voice asked for the number he wished. Heavens! His had been 'J.' The handle was extremely thick and refused to fit snugly in his palm. It was heavy, had a very short cord, and he couldn't see a plate for a number. Holding it, he thought he smelled unfiltered cigarette smoke and heard some wise- guy telling his date he was catching the next streetcar to her house.

He stood there, holding the antique, thinking about trying to call every friend he had in every corner of the globe. It was a wonderful way to show his heartfelt need to bury the institution among the ashes of its greed and selfishness. If he could not reverse charges, perhaps he could use an expired credit card. Then, he noticed the three tiny buttons, invisible 'til then because of darkness.

He ducked his head an*d read the number on each. 704.* He thought, *this might be the Italian number for information.* Slowly he hit them, hearing a ponderous clicking and clanging as he pressed each one. There was another long pause and then a ring.

It rang four times. Then there was a click and he sensed he was about to get a recorded announcement, or worse, a menu, so he hung up. He was about to leave when words flooded his thoughts. *Me and five billion other lunatics chasing God down narrow deserted streets; Blinded by the mist His angles left.*

He decided to try again. Perhaps it was that line, or perhaps something he had no control over. *704?* He began running down the alphabet. Seven was 'G' and zero was 'O' and that made four 'D.' Put that all together and to Norris it spelled excitement.

He dialed and it rang four times again. Then, the click, and then, the most tantalizing recorded announce-ment he'd ever waited for came on:

GOOD AFTERNOON. YOU HAVE REACHED GOD. UNFORTUNATELY ALL HIS LINES ARE PRESENTLY BUSY. YOU MAY CHOOSE TO HANG UP AND TRY AGAIN OR YOU MAY CONTINUE TO HOLD. YOUR CALL WILL BE ANSWERED IN ORDER. IN ANY CASE, GOD THANKS YOU FOR CALLING.

The taped music was soft—softer than clouds. He thought he'd heard it before and loved it for a long time. Gently, his foot began tapping. He nodded his head and waited. Then, a series of menus began in every conceivable language. He recognized the French, German, Dutch, Spanish, Italian and he thought, Russian. He could understand enough of the first four to tell it was the same announcement. Once the Asian ones began, he started to think of the question he wanted to open with.

"Say God. They claim You can do anything in the world. So, can you make a rock you can't pick up? Ha ha ha ha! ... Very cleaver no? NO!!!" he yelled into the phone. "You king-sized jerk," he muttered. "You're going to speak with God, and you want to be a wise guy?"

So, he fell back on questions he admired about the subject. Like Einstein's comment;

*If God made the universe, it may be that he had little choice in what it could be made from, only what He would put in* it. Then again, *I do not believe God played dice with the universe.* That should get some thought he announced to the dark, which was somehow not as dense. While the really foreign languages purred on, he thought again. *What about life on other planets? Is man the ultimate? Are we going to get better and do bigger things?* He thought he was getting better. Then there was a different kind of silence on the line.

"YES, MAY I HELP YOU?"

The tone seemed to demand he remove his shoes. It was more than a voice. It was the clouds and sky speaking; the trees telling Norris about Nature's perfection. He opened his mouth but nothing came forth. He swallowed, then gasped and was still mute. He yawned and threw his lower jaw to and fro and still nothing.

"I AM UNABLE TO GRANT YOU MORE TIME. YOU MAY REDIAL AT YOUR PLEASURE."

Then, there was absolute, totally, shining silence, as Street watched a pin point of light slowly expand until it filled the booth. Quietly he placed the phone back and stepped free. No … stepped into total quandary.

Ten steps down the marble floors and he instantly knew the only question anyone should ever want God to answer. He had been such a tongue-tied fool!

He turned and charged back to the niche still filled with blackness. It was a huge empty and balanced blackness which defied description. Silently, he saw the woman race by, her leather wrappings making a merry laughing sound. Then, Cindy stepped up, arm in arm with the two Spanish damsels to cluck their tongues and shake their heads in total disbelief.

His mother appeared next. He had to shut his eyes and keep them closed so he missed the disappointment in her eyes …but he heard her voice. *You had such a wonderful opportunity, Street. You should have cut your hair. You have such pretty eyes.*

"What the hell is going on here?" he asked the blackness. "I must be mad!" Then he thought that perhaps this was a natural state of mind after such an encounter. He decided he had to leave immediately, but before he did he asked the only question all of us really want answered. 'Is there really an afterlife and how long does it last?' but now there wasn't a booth, a heavy phone. Not even a recorded announcement. So it didn't count.

On the way out he went over to one of the gaudy Baroque main side chapels, where five separate tourist groups intently listening to their guides. There were four languages going on at the same time and all the Babel made him long for the telephone booth. He returned to what he thought was the exact spot and it still was not there.

This time he felt along the wall then got down on his hands and knees to feel for any traces of its outline. There was exactly nothing. A couple crossed themselves as they passed him. Two girls snickered. He got up and this time returned to the square and the afternoon sunlight.

He sat on the church steps for almost an hour. Then, he carefully worked his way back to where the woman was. She was gone.

Street asked at least fifteen loiterers one by one. Half of them claimed to have been there all day and not one of them could remember seeing a woman like her.

He stood very still as slowly Saint Peter's, both the Square and the Basilica, became as empty as he could ever imagine them. Almost as empty as he seemed to feel just then ... so empty, he thought he would float off into the insanely, blue Italian afternoon sky. When he took his first step, he knew it was too late for that also.

# Let's Have Another Cup Of Coffee

The first body had four raggedly edged dark spots across its back. When the corpse was turned over on his back, he looked to be in his middle teens. Two dark soggy spots also appeared on the front of the frayed but otherwise clean shirt.

"There's two more over here," Street had announced in an unmistakable Maryland slur. As he made this flat tone announcement, he leaned down and futilely brushed at the colonies of flies clustered about the dried blood stains. Annoyed the ants decided to challenge and won. As he offered, "Looks like this one over here is the father and the other one's the Momma."

"All shot for the Yankee Dollar," a medium sized blonde grunted. "Wonder if there's any more of their mates further on." His Aussie accent was becoming nearly smothered as he edged into the tangled vines and undergrowth surrounding the simple bamboo shack.

Right then Street Norris was amazed how the windshield morphed into a large screen. He shook his head but the actors refused to vanish. His projection looked very different

"Let's hope there ain't any mates of the ones who murdered these. And Arnie, it ain't the dollar that did 'em in, it's the coffee. Ain't that so, Norris?" The oldest of the trio, the bearded, thickly set one with the many times broken nose, nodded agreement.

"Yes." he told the screen's trio, "Coffee, at least the beans grown in these tropical highlands, bringing top dollar, was why his trio was currently tramping the Guatemala Highlands, the next to last decade of the Twentieth Century. The reason why each of them carried illegal Glock automatic, holstered beneath loose fitting shirts. Also the reason for the semi-automatic rifles stuffed in one side of each large cloth saddle bag each of the trio of sour smelling burro reluctantly carried.

Ten years before cotton and bananas had been the major crops in this country. They were both grown on the coastal plain and sold to American manufacturers. Then coffee was a secondary crop, mostly for domestic consumption until Juan Valdez, and his photogenic burro became the icon for the coffee grown in the cool highlands of Columbia, and also became the almost instant choice for American businessmen.

Guatemala not only had mountains to produce this type bean, but also a landed aristocracy wanting more money for shopping sprees in Miami or Madrid. However, their highlands were inhabited by Indians who had been forced into that cold dampness by the Spanish invaders over three centuries ago. Even so, it still looked like a simple project to move in, and just use the judges and courts to claim the Indians were squatters, confiscate their lands, and add to their already generous fortunes.

It looked fool proof five Jesuit priests turned these simple plans to acquire the area on its ear. When the initial legal probes began, the quintet made extensive searches through their nearly four centuries old church archives. Lo and behold! They found the original land grants issued by the King of Spain, giving legal title to the land to the Indians.

The landed gentry were not discouraged so easily. If they could not force the owners off by legal manipulations, they would use whatever force necessary to gain control. The murders began just a little over four months later.

At first it was a slight of hand thing. Only the tribal elders and leaders were shot, fell from steep cliffs, or were run over by wayward trucks. When this had little or no effect, the educated few joined the growing lists of corpses. When this also failed to give the gentry control of the sloping, well-watered terraces, the killings spread to individual farmers, and then to their families and workers. And when this too failed to persuade the stubborn ones, one morning two of the priests were found dead with their faces mutilated, their limbs hacked off, and each nailed to a separate palm tree.

Most of this was kept out of the local papers. The three gringos arrived only when it was discovered that hunting permits to shoot Indians were being sold for $3,000.00 to rich Europeans and some South American millionaires. Each permit allowed three kills, which were explained by the police and military as self-defense. Later this held some water since a few of the younger Indians had decided to fight fire with fire, and acquired some old fashioned single shot firearms.

Two weeks before he stood over the parent's corpses, two terrified Dutch travelers had informed a member of his Co-op, *'While we were having a drink at a five star hotel in the capitol, we actually overheard four upper-level police officers bragging about how many permits they had sold to shot Indians that week!'*

Five days after this, Street met Ian Maynard Lawless, at the International Airport. Ian, who always signed as I. M. Lawless, was only too eager to get *Up in them thar hills and do some* hunting *on our own, partner!*

Ian's average size belied his incredible physical strength and endurance. Stripped, his muscles were layers like rock strata. And he also possessed a cat-like balance, quickness and grace which he usually managed to conceal until it was needed. His political view was basic. *Take any Pol and dump him in a foreign land and as long as he can speak the lingo, he'll not only be right at home, and accepting graft in less than a week.*

The second member arrived later the same day Lawless showed. Arnold Whitlow Hargrove, was a fifth degree *Black Belt* who could really chop concrete blocks to bits and snatch flies from the air with a pair of chop sticks. But those were his basic skills. Norris once watched in rapt, amazed admiration as Arnie cleaned out a Mexican bar featuring four knife wielders. In just about the same length of time it would take to describe his moves, there were eight senseless bodies, some with multi broken bones scattered about. Arnie's only scar was a torn sleeve on his light tan, hand tailored, Harris Tweed sports coat.

Once they booked a house in a very upper middle class sector, it took another two days to assemble a Ford 150 truck, and sufficiently bribe some airport office to release their armament. *Then they headed into them thar hills.*

"So here we go again," Lawless half leered, as he nosed about the edges of the beaten down grounds. "Gonna be a damned nice feeling removing some old, dedicated Nazis."

AIan we aren't a humanitarian death squad."

"Yeah so you always claim. And I'm ready to admit, most of the time we never start out butY," Ian retorted, and winked at

Arnold, whose greatest asset was his emotional control always registered a constant nil on his face meter.

"We're up here to set up a system to move the Indians who want to go, over to Chiapas."

"Where the corrupt Mexicans can exploit them the same as always." Ian retorted again.

"Yes, Ian, dammit. But they're not gonna be hunted."

"So don't fret," Arnie interrupted. "You can be sure once we can clear the non- combatants out of here, the war can really get started."

"Right …And we'll miss all the fun again! Soon as the good shit comes down, you'll be back lecturing strung out freshmen Econ majors and Arnie will be back building sanitation plants in Oz's Outback." Ian grunted before adding," I wonder what part of a human you take back to hang on your wall, Street?"

"Nice." Norris almost let it go. "More like where the hell could you hang it?"

That got a chuckle, before Street added, "Forget the body parts Ian. Once this is over, Ian Maynard Lawless will be get shipped back to the stunning rural loveliness of New Jersey," Norris snorted and Arnie laughed. Street's tone modified and got much softer, slightly deadly

. "We'll do what we have to do, Ian. No more, no less," and though he did not say it Norris silently appended, And *you'll be the one I can trust. Arnie's always been the random X factor in this outfit.*

"Well we have arms." Arnie offered, his flat tone falling to the tightly packed earth like a spent cat.

"Just what we got with us."

"Any C3 to C4 coming through the pipe line, Street?"

"No Ian… just plenty of Gringo dollars to bribe the border boys on both sides." That brought the Lawless sardonic screech he claimed to be laughter and a slight nod from, *The Killing Machine.* As Street silently spoke, his unlisted nick name for Arnold, he thought, *I got all the complications I need already.*

He knew what they both had in mind as they buried the bodies beneath a slim layer of black earth and a thick one of red sand stones. He also realized that all he could do was try and limit their responses. Norris also had a tiny tinge of doubt that if and when that came, did he really wanted to limit them?

Especially when Lawless flipped the ragged sheet over the young kid's face before they began throwing the red, moist soil on it.

When they got to the Mexican Guatemalan border, Street took care of the price for each border violation. *The Fine* was established at $115.00 for each adult male, $75.00 for each female and $45.00 for children under 14.

While Street made the two day trip, there and back, Ian spent his time mapping three major routes through the mountains into San Cristobel de Las Cruses, the capital of the Mexican state Chiapas.

Route **A** was very strenuous but avoided all the hot spots on both sides. It was intended for known and active trouble makers. **B** route was of medium physical difficulty and also for the lesser violent avoid possible interdiction and additional >fines=, by local police. The last was for the elderly and youngsters.

When Street returned, Arnold quietly informed him he planned gathering a few militants at a time and training them to become scouts; defenders only as a last resort. "It's gonna take at least six well trained and absolutely loyal cadres of nine men each, Street." Norris silently fretted about the time that was going to consume.

All told, this took almost ten months, or 143 more murders before they could begin transporting. After the first two dozen, five of them children and eight mothers, Street was unable and unwilling to prevent Ian and Arnie from disappearing from time to time. They never stayed more than two nights and swore to him they never crossed into Mexico. Street read the box scores in the weekly newspaper one of the local store owners kept on his counter. After eight months the score was 853 for the home team and 53 for the visitors. But the low score featured police commanders, corrupt judges, and a few federal administrators. When the three remaining priest were found in the town trash heap after the local rat colonies had an overnight feast, Street joined them. The visitor's score reached 92 and the home team stayed almost static after the federal pigs were done.

Three heavy gun shots echoed and re-echoed across the mountain valley as Lawless went prone and stared up at Arnie, perched half way up a large densely leafed tree. Arnie swung his field glasses in the direction of the shot's birth place. After a minute or so, there was weaker single shot. Street waited while Arnie dismounted and motioned toward the east.

Fifteen minutes later he held the glasses and spat out a quiet string of anger. When he had some self-control he whispered, "There's three of 'em, Ian. One of them's a cop. Can't tell if he's from here or Mexico. The other two are wearing ski masks." He handed Arnie the glasses and continued. It was their last week and the home team was *suddenly very active.*

"There's three bodies hanging by their feet. Just like dead deer. And the fucking cop's taking pictures." Arnie took one short sighting and moved off. Ian followed. Street came last. They moved as silently as Jaguars. It took ten minutes to get in position for a shot.

They dropped onto their bellies, just shy of the mound's crest. It took about fifteen seconds for Street to point out whose target was whose. He chose the cop. Arnie got the taller of the two masked hunters. Ian gave him a slight grin as he adjusted his position and sighted in. Norris was dead certain Ian didn't have any preference. He lifted his sighting eye long enough to be sure everyone was zeroed in before he gave the muttered command.

Three slight non-echoing coughs came half a heartbeat after all three targets recoiled and fell. Norris waited a full two minutes, using the telescopic sight to monitor any movements. Then he rose and took two or three steps toward the bodies before Ian's hand grabbed a shoulder.

"Let's get the hell outta here, Norris."

"Go to hell, Lawless. I'm going over there."

"Me too, Ian." Lawless gave them both a sardonic smile and led the way.

While Ian unmasked the hunters, Arnie fished for their passports. "They're both Russians," he announced and handed Street the passports.

"Ukraine," Street amended. "Kiev, the capitol."

He paused. "AIan, get that camera. Run the whole roll. And get the fucking ski masks off before you . . ."

"Street, the cop's from here. Take him too?" Street nodded.

"Yeah. Then we'll send them back to their home addresses and see if any more of them want . . .."

"Great idea," Arnie grunted and began stripping the masks. In a week it was obvious from no further reports that the home team ceased operations again.

Once their operation was fully active, the trio cleared out and a new team of seven men and three women took charge.

Two years past and almost 12,000 Indians were moved into Mexico where their weaving talents were totally exploited. The *Ricos* took over the abandoned fincas and Guatemalan Coffee became a fixture in the overcharging coffee houses which suddenly began expanding into American Suburbia.

For a time, the hunting permits were outrageously expensive, but then the demand ceased. The murders still went on, so two of the surviving priests who had stayed clear of the original effort to save the region, took off their religious gear, and went into the surrounding mountains to become weapons and demolition experts. Eventually when they needed funds to continue, they accepted them from the Mexican Drug Cartels who saw a double opportunity for new markets as well as increased acreage.

It was the first week in June, over three years since Street had pulled out of the highlands. It was mutually agreed that Guatemala City would be his and Ian's departure point for Peru. As always he checked into the *Pension Swizzes*, directly opposite to the vehicle entrance to the National Police Headquarters. He was a few days early, so he took his meals at the hotel, and for the most part stayed in his air conditioned apartment. If he did venture out, it was always late at night.

The evening of Ian's second day past his ETA, Street started making useless and expensive long distance calls. He was about to confirm his flight for the next day and assume Ian would join him in Lima when a quiet knock sent a current of dread through his hand as he responded. Ian was supported by the pension's porter and an attractive woman who eagerly gave up her end of the burden.

While Street helped place Ian on the other bed, she disappeared behind the bathroom door. He gave the porter a large tip, as she reappeared. She hadn't been too successful washing his blood from her loosely fitting beige blouse. Street heard the door close as he turned his full attention to Ian's damages.

Once he had Ian's shirt loosened he could see that the blood was mostly coming from where four of his back teeth, two to a side, had recently been knocked out. He got a wet towel and their first aid kit. There was a small but deep gash along the chin. It was deep enough so Street saw bone as he examined it.

Norris began cleaning the wound. "Not too much!" Ian managed before the pain drowned any other words. Street gave him a pen and tablet when he motioned he wanted to speak. As Ian scribbled, Street used his fingers to close the gap and one by one snap four Band-Aid stitches over the wound. Lawless thrust the pad under his nose as he finished. His handwriting resembled a retarded fourth grader.

*Get out of here. Know you're here. In here! Told me we got four hours,* he wrote.

"They do this? "Lawless frowned, but took the pad back and began scribbling.

*Yeah. Hammer. Decked me good. Gonna kill me look. Head pig asked how it felt. Said pretty good for a little teen age girl. Got 'em. Laughed...threw me in the street. Thought I was mucho macho.*

Then the pain won again. Ian blinked and tried not to breathe too deeply as Street gently rubbed at the caked blood. He quickly surrendered there and started in on Ian's hands, and then he replaced the white and gold cow boy shirt with one of his own. Ian's pain seemed to lessen.

You're marked. Ought-ta go. Now. Screw the clothes. Get a cab, he scribbled and sat up.

Less than two hours later they were in First Class on a K.L.M. plane headed for Dallas, Texas. They had stopped long enough for a doctor to compliment Street on his efforts, then put eleven stitches in the gash and give Ian something for the pain. Now he was cleaned up and wearing Street's shirt and slacks which looked like ill matched tents on his lean frame.

As always the Dutch asked no questions and required no I.D. The captain told Street they could pay the fare once they landed and his friend had, "Proper medical attention."

After a further check at a Texas hospital, and a new prescription was issued, they caught a late evening flight for Washington, D.C. By then Ian could speak almost normally.

"So weren't we the successful mission? Good God damn thing we don't work for Uncle Sam. We'd have medals for this screw up," he offered.

"You looked really sexy with lots of blood on you. Especially after I got you into my duds, dude."

"I'll bet. That Dutch babe almost crapped in her Bikini underwear when I got thrown at her."

"But she got you off the sidewalk before someone pissed all over you. Typically a nice Dutch lady."

"Yeah, guess so." He paused and then before Street could prevent it, he unloaded.

"The bastard who used that hammer on me was the brother of some pig we did in, Street. Wanted to beat me to death, but the boss liked my guts. Did let the little prick tap my other cheek though.'

He paused, half smiled at a passing attendant. It slithered into the edges of the large bandage.

"The Indians are still being murdered. The pigs on both sides of the border probably retired on what was paid 'em. Nobody in Valhalla's boycotting mountain grown Guatemalan coffee. The priests are now dealing in drugs and both you and me are *Persona non Grata*. That's my third country. How many for you? Eight?"

"Same number as you. But there's a couple good things Ian."

"Name just one."

"Only had nine murders so far this year, and we helped 12,000 or so innocents get one whole border nearer to the Promised Land."

"Yeah and let's hope most of the teenagers we got over are already there."

"Employed."

"Yeah. You want that super-sized?"

"Even so that's better than, ***Where do you want me to shoot you first?'***"

"Okay for Christ sake! Enough! How about letting this wounded warrior get some shut eye?"

Norris nodded and turned to the window. Gentle snores filled his ears as he took in the clouds. There were some fascinating formations. One looked exactly like an applauding clown. He winked and nodded, and put his hand over to feel Ian's pulse. Remarkably it was almost normal.

# For Lovers and Sluggers

Saturday morning coffee at The Duke's residence was always served with homemade bread, four different marmalades, jellies and preserves and legions of fleas. Nellie, his one true love for fourteen years, baked the bread, Duke cooked the toppings and the nine cat, three dog animal colony supplied the fleas free of charge. Even with the fleas, those were Saturday mornings Barry Oman hated to miss, unless he had some serious business which could not be ignored or postponed. This particular Saturday the fleas were so aggressive and abundant, he and Duke had their feet on the coffee table, avoiding their most serious assaults.

Duke's real name was Harold Kubrick Novinger. His recent voluntarily abandoned profession was architect. He once held that position in a very prestigious firm. His family was members of the social as well as political elite in our nation's capital, and his only brother had died from an overdose of various concoctions of erotic drugs three years before.

Duke and Barry were enjoying a few cups of aromatic and exotic coffee, three types of bread and a large jar of cherry preserves. However, above all they were engaged in enjoying each other's company.

For the less gifted, conversation with could pose an almost insurmountable obstacle. The Duke's conversa-tional talent was plagued with a considerable time warp when it came to oral engagements. His answers usually lagged a full two minutes or more behind the questions. Duke's 1500 or so LSD trips, along with the fact he also accompanied acid with about a weekly ounce of high-grade marijuana for the last fourteen years accounted for this unique disability.

To the uninitiated it appeared he was not paying the least bit of attention to their words, or he didn't possess the intelligence to follow the gist of their conversations. In both cases such assumptions were not only entirely incorrect, but usually gave Duke decided advantages. He was listening and he was very intelligent. Simply put, his thought processes were usually working on a totally different plane, which a more normal person would consider insanity.

For the last few years there was a persistent rumor circulating that he had discovered a large sum money while cultivating some rented land on the extreme northern borders of Montgomery County, Maryland. If so, he never admitted to that. However, for the last three years he had made no effort to work, or deal drugs for profit. He lived in a very nice house in the best section of Takoma Park, paid a lawn service to manicure its yard and extensive flower garden, and drove a fairly new Ford truck.

Of his three other constant companions, only Nellie Atwood held a regular job. The other two, Jeffery Robert Feldman and Nancy, Nellie's younger sister, made no pretense of working. Yet, they too had enough money to survive nicely among the middle-class level into which each had been born.

There were two other occupants in this nine room brick home, set well back from a tree lined street near the Capitol Beltway. There were always at least two boarders, or refugees as Jeff and Nancy labeled them, wherever Duke lived. The current duo rented two adjoining rooms on the upper floor and was employed carpenters. The man was a union journeyman, and his girlfriend was his helper.

Even when attired in a pair of paint-splattered coveralls, Carroll was absolutely stunningly beautiful. When she cared to use just a minimum amount of cosmetics, and attired in something more form-fitting she could, Oman noted, *Stop traffic in all four directions in the middle of a blizzard.*

Just then it was early May and everything was wakening after a terrible winter of snow, sleet and freezing rain which had blanketed the area for almost three solid months. Once that reluctantly surrendered and began to melt, there had been another two weeks of general flooding. Now, all that was gone and Duke had just finished planting his small herb and veggie garden at the extreme rear of the property. By mid-summer there would be fresh tomatoes, squash, onions, and beans which he would sell or give to his friends and their friends, if there was abundance.

Earlier, he had lamented how much he wanted to get his hands in some rich soil now that the sun was beginning to dissipate the morning chill. Just then, they were sprawled on a sagging sofa, speaking of fools and the egotistical errors of self-proclaimed kings, but mostly they were dwelling upon the fools.

"So you really think that Donald Trump can win another term, Duke?"

"Lots of worms this year. Means the soil is really ready for some heavy use."

"Maybe we're stupid enough to elect movie stars as Congressmen and Senators, even Governors, but are we now stupid enough to reelect a failed gambling entrepreneur, basically a liar and impaired dyslexic President?"

"I got a theory. Colder it is, the more fat they grow, like on Polar Bears."

"Hell, Trump is so far to the right, he thinks we have no racial problems because he had none when he grew up in preps schools and at good old Penn."

When Duke continued staring out the distant picture window, Barry embellished his scorn. "Well, except for the tall or heavy black jocks. And Duke, I'm positive the entire family has one form of dyslexia or another. I think he claims being born again cured his. God gets blame and credit for anything as long as … Hell with it."

"I had to push some of the biggest ones out of the way to plant the squash. Biggest damn worms I've seen in ten years."

"I'm not sure we're all going to hell in a hand cart, but I 'm worried about the religious right electing someone even worse than *The Donald*."

"Barry, there's some real shit coming down from the right. Ronnie Ray-Gun just made us feel more secure about our prejudices, you know? If this man running for president is a bigot, I mean what the hell … So can we, right? Bet your ass I am."

He knew that Duke had once threatened to write an essay which would expose all the layers of misconceptions the nation labored under. He wanted to title it, *Bet Your Ass Writings and Musings.*

"You read that Ronnie Ray-Gun never really cared if there was an atomic war while he was the Prez? I heard he thought if there was, all the true believers were going to be raptured right up to Heaven and not suffer at all! I wonder if they go clothes and all, or naked as their God made them?"

Duke's grin almost lit the room.

"We had Prohibition when only twenty-percent of the country voted for it. We could get God for less. But God still isn't as popular as hooch, Barry."

"Duke, you got to do something about these fleas! Even with my feet up here, they're still jumping up off the rugs and getting me good!"

Oman reached out and scratched his ankles for almost a full minute while Duke contemplated the shafts of sunlight coming through the double French doors leading to the back yard and his garden.

"Duke, the trouble with God is He wants you to sing whether it's good or bad times." "We got more problems than we can deal with. Most of us don't even want to deal with the ones threatening to kill us. Not unless they can be erased or solved in ten days, Barry."

Just as he was about to join Duke at his chosen juncture, the female boarder came down the stairs and she was not wearing her overalls. Both men stopped to admire her Hollywood lushness trying to spill out from all areas of her green, silk, dressing gown. Her development was so firm and sculpted under the fabric the two embroidered red dragons across its front were ready to leap right off the fabric.

"Religious fanatics are only one group we gotta rid ourselves of if we are ever gonna have a decent world," Duke pronounced, not taking his eyes off the woman as she reached the foot of the stairs. "I vote that preachers, teachers, and parents go first. They're the ones preventing us from having a decent world, believe me."

Barry was about to offer his own over-simplistic solution to all problems; which was to take one Supreme Court Justice, two Senators, ten Congressmen, and two Cabinet members and threaten to machine gun them on the steps of the capitol. When they surrendered, it would be announced that no one could retire or resign, and if things were not better in six months, there would be another lottery, and this time …

That all just jammed itself to a stop somewhere halfway up his throat to his lips. When the woman reached the bottom of the steps, she had to make a half-turn to get to the kitchen. The shock came when he got a good look at her left eye. To say it was a black eye would be like saying the National Debt was just an economic illusion.

It looked like an overripe plum about to explode from inner pressures. A dark purple knob raised at least an-half-an-inch and extended from the edge of her nose to her ear lobe. The eye was still partially visible through a veil of blackish, red-laced blood. It looked like it was about to fall right out onto her cheek if anyone looked too closely or spoke too loudly.

"Extremists are better off out where at least we can still laugh at 'em," Duke intoned. "Gotta laugh 'em right off the stage … otherwise they go underground and turn into Hitlers and begin undermining the entire house of cards."

Oman felt so guilty, he almost leaped from his seat to assist her.

When she nodded and said, "Good morning. How are you all?" in a voice which seemed to wrap around his entire body, Street's pornographic illusions paused. However, his eyes continued to follow her until she disappeared into the kitchen.

"What the hell happens when we get a totally new concept, Oman? Four things," Duke said holding up five fingers.

"We ridicule it and hope it leaves. And when it don't, we ignore it. And when it still hangs around, we make it either illegal or immoral … Sometimes both.  And when that don't work, we end up worshiping the goddamn thing. Can't we learn that was the process everything we now declare essential had to go through?"

"Jesus H. Christ," Barry muttered, and took the last of his coffee as he ignored the fleas.

"We Americans are always looking for the *panacea*. Want our problems solved instantly, either by a person with the answers in a book we can buy, or even better, a pill we can just swallow."

The woman was gone, so the fleas returned. Oman reached out and began scratching again, while he let the shock set in and waited for it to dissolve.

Meanwhile, Nellie came in from the kitchen with another tray of rye bread and three wedges of cheese. She was the only one who liked cheese with her breakfast. She had the build of a good high school football lineman. In fact Nell looked like she could lead down field blocking on the best team Oman ever ran the ball.

But the athletic parts of her ended there. She was a bank clerk who stayed at her job, so she could read. Nellie read anything she could find from Kant to the comics. There were piles of books everywhere. Usually, they could be divided into three stacks. Books Nellie had read. Books she wanted to read and books she wanted to give to others or trade for more books.

For fourteen years they had been the perfect couple physically. Duke was almost as tall as Oman, and he weighed about 60 pounds more than Oman's 225. Duke and Nellie could take up the entire sofa with not an inch to spare.

Since neither she nor her mate seemed at all surprised by the condition of the female boarder, Oman felt compelled to bring it to their attention. However, right then, he could not devise a means of politely interrupting Duke's dissertation.

"Want to clear up the ecology?"

All Duke's questions were rhetorical.

"Make every one of the sons-a-bitches who are either CEO'S or owners live within two- hundred yards of their plants and make them drink the well water." This brought a burst of laughter from Nellie.

"Really want clean air? Stop everyone under thirty-five from driving. Don't like that solution? Good. Make it everyone over the age of forty can't drive, and charge fifty dollars a day to park anywhere inside the economic zone of every city. All those choices too hard … Fine … tax everyone five-grand a year for every empty seat in their cars when they do the daily commute."

"God, you're in rare form today," Nell offered as she was about to take her cheese and books to her room.

"Right," Duke smiled. "Simple answers for complex problems. Elect The Duke and disconnect your water filters in a month."

"Duke?"

"What?"

"Barry, it really isn't any of our business." Nellie offered.

Then, as she headed for the stairway, the woman came back through the room carrying a large tray with two cups of coffee, a plate of bagels and three large jars of various jellies. She nodded again and as she followed Nellie, Oman was reminded of a noblewoman and her lady in waiting. He fixated on them as they slowly, majestically ascended the stairs.

"Nell doesn't believe in engagement or confron-tation, does she?"

"There's nothing can be done about the goddamn fleas, man. Every time I think we got 'em cleaned up, either Jeff or Nancy get into their animal oppression. You let all these cats and dogs have a free run and you get kittens, puppies, and fleas. It's just natural. And Nell won't hear about using a chemical to flush them out. You can protect yourself, but you can't oppress the animals! She says it ain't natural. She really believes that as a species, we've risen to where we are on the backs and hides of oppressed animals, children and ugly, which blends perfectly with the dark complexions or fat women!"

"Duke?"

"Okay, maybe once we domesticate an animal, we can't oppress it. But who the hell can claim cats are domesticated? Not me!"

"What's going on?"

"Fleas are natural. I read a great poem once. *Fleas! Adam Had Em!*" and Duke roared at his successful effort to remember.

"Does she always have one of those? This isn't the first time I've seen her marked. But this one's a masterpiece. What the hell do you think makes a woman as beautiful, as delicious as her put up with crap like that?"

"Limit the freedom of cats and dogs and you can curtail the attacks of fleas. It's that simple."

"I mean, look how gorgeous she is. She could go out and get anything she wanted. And she stays with a pig like this? Give me one good reason for that?"

"Of course Nell and Nancy would love to bring wild animals in here. Bring wounded wild animals right in off the streets and domesticate them while they heal their wounds. Hell, they have been bringing wounded men and wild animals in here since I started bedding them. Just a natural thing for both of them, I guess."

"Duke! She looks so bad I want to take her over to the hospital before her eye falls out and she goes blind!"

"You've never really met Harry and Jean, have you? Couple of real ding-bats if you ask me. Work their butts off doing carpentry all week then they hole up all week-end. We never see 'em. 'Cept when they want to buy or trade some weed. See 'em plenty then."

"So why does she take that abuse?"

Duke was not inclined to offer an explanation and he was definitely not ready to volunteer to take her to the *Seventh Day Adventist Hospital*.

"Hospital is more than likely closed right now, Barry, and I don't hold much with doctors and hospitals anyway since they killed my brother. Bunch of body mechanics who're really overpaid if you ask me."

"Duke, Jesus Christ! She's really hurt this time."

"You know, I've thought about broads that good-looking. I mean I might toss Nell over for something that good. I've caught myself wondering why she hangs on to a guy as evil as Harry."

"And, so?"

"Well, I can only think of one answer for that." Oman did not interject a single word and gave thanks that for once he was right on The Duke's wave length at the same time.

"It's really simple. All complex problem's got simple solutions or answers. And Barry, the simple answer here is that..."

When the Duke stopped abruptly and began staring out into the backyard again, Oman almost screamed, "Well, what the hell is it? Come back to earth man! Tell me what's so damned simple to explain ..."

*"I guess he just can't hit her hard enough."*

# Nightmare of Black on White: A Trilogy

## Part One: Dissonance

Grace Norris waited until the Buick sedan's back door was closed before she delivered a resounding open palm slap on her youngest son's cheek. "Don't ever, do you hear me! Don't you ever let me see you doing this again!" Then she pushed his hands aside and slapped the other cheek just as intensely. She also smothered his request for why he was getting this with, "We'll just wait and let your father explain why. But I can tell you this! You will never, do you hear me, never come down here again. He was ready to duck, perhaps even catch another slap but it did not come. Instead his mother scalded him with, "What will the neighbors think if they see you doing this?" Street Norris was very disappointed that Aunt Lillian Mae Dowers, the Buick's owner and his favorite adult beside his two older brothers made no effort to interfere or comment.

His court martial was ordered right after dinner. It was convened as soon as his father finished his dessert and listened intently to the indictment. When his mother ceased hissing and glaring at her husband, Wilhelm Norris wiped his lips with a freshly starched and ironed napkin and ordered his son into the sun pallor. The family's three hundred year old record of Prussian professional military service was further accented when the commander sat on the caned sofa pausing to adjust the monocle in his right eye. It continued when he ordered Street to close the only door so his wife and her two maiden sisters, crowded at its threshold, could not hear or witness Wilhelm's judgment and sentence.

Street's commanding officer wasted no time rendering that once the door was secured. He almost whispered the verdict.

"Your mother informed me that she found you playing with the blacks over on Cold Spring Lane, Street." As his youngest and strangest son began to nod Wilhelm pronounced his decision. "This must stop immediately. But, Street, not for the reason she gave. What our neighbors think or their opinions of us is of no interest to me. But peace within the confines of my home does. So, in order for there to be peace, you are not to play with the black boys again. You must, however, also know that you never despise or hate someone because they are members of some other race, ethnicity, nationality, or religion. You understand when you go through that door you must be certain that the only time you will reprise to another is because they have insulted or threatened you as an individual. You deal only with the individual, not the group. Do you understand?"

All Street could do was nod, but he was not allowed to tell his judge this had already been drilled into him since he was old enough to understand its complexities. All he could do was wait to see if there was any immediate punishment, and heave a silent Thank You to the gods of chance as his father reached for his evening cigar signifying the court martial was over and he was obliged to accept its renderings without question and with blind obedience.

His mother pushed past him when he opened the door. Street was positive she would not be either happy of satisfied with his punishment. Besides, he knew that his Father was not the least interested in his reasons and would more than likely have shaken his head and grunted if Street had tried to explain. No matter what the facts were, once he sat on his bed he remained confused, angry so he offered his case to the *Bat Man* comic book cover air plane glued to the back of his door.

"I wanted to play with guys as good and as fast as me, for Christ sake! That's all! Jesus! The last two years up on the playground I'm the fastest guy there. Even faster than Bootie and that's fast! So the only way they'll let me play touch football is I get John Dent to throw and Dutch Jones to center it and try and block out four or five guys, since they play eight or nine on us! The last time it was ten, and we had to spot 'em points! And even then I caught almost everything thrown out there. I'm just too fast! Street was certain *Bat Man* nodded he understood.

But down there with the blacks, and no one asked me to tell them they're all the college professors' kids... that they go to a private school and smart! No one wants to hear any of that shit. Kind ah gives…at least four of 'em are fast as me! And one might beat me…it's a fairer game and it's more fun! And now I gotta go back to the other crap! Even when we win, all we get is another pile of crap about how I shouldn't be allowed to go out more than ten yards…What the hell can I do? I gotta listen to my Old Man! He was a major in the German army in the war. Demands respect…Even my brothers don't give him any crap and they're both over twenty-one Batman didn't interrupt, didn't ask any questions and never blinked an eye, but he also didn't criticize or rebuke his argument either.

## Part Two: Adagio

Even after mid-night the Baltimore August was still hazy hot. The oppressive humidity almost made Street Norris ignore the five slouching males as they turned the corner. However, that ceased the instant he was aware they were forming a rough semi-circle facing him. Even so he was slightly amused they all had long greased back Duck Tail haircuts with curls along their collar lines. That coincided with the rest of their matched ensemble. Their light, tan, tightly pegged at the ankles slacks were freshly pressed and bore no stains, or repairs. All this uniformity raised an unfamiliar quandary for Norris. *Which face are you gonna have to have change before they'd realize I'm not going to be harassed, threatened or bullied?*

He was about to begin his junior year at Maryland University, majoring in economics. His employment at Eastern Stainless Steel was just a summer interim, a nest egg to carry him over until the first GI Bill check arrived sometime in October. This was his last day on the 3pm to 11:30pm shift. The Graveyard as his crew members called it since the hours almost ruined both all normal day and night activities. Street was following his routine, which was a long bus ride from the plant to Highland- Town in time to catch the last Cross Town bus, and then another long street car ride before he reached Hamilton in the Northern suburbs. *It's the shortest of the quintet. He's the boss...* he decided with as much emotion as he used scanning the front page of *The Baltimore Sun Paper*.

The bus stop fronted an always vacant lot protected by a twelve feet chain link fence. The only life he had ever seen in there was an occasional stray cat looking for a mouse or rat. Western Maryland Dairy used an area to his right to store their heavy milk cases. They went six high except for the one nearest, which was only four and the top case held nine empty quart bottles. He helped himself to two, eased them behind his back and waited while the quintet completed its maneuver. They looked very menacing but Street did not feel like they were Sioux or he was Custer. Just as he wondered why one of them hadn't opened the engagement the opening salvo whipped across his brow.

"Hey…what cha yuh up to Bud? Who the hell told yuh yuh could be on our corner?" the tallest snarled, rocking in tempo on his double soled and heeled black and white wing tips." Yuh lookin for trouble asshole?" Street's silence and calm brought, "Well, yuh done got it."

"Billy! He's got ah couple bottles behind him!" the medium-sized almost Albino on Street's left hissed. "No shit, Bill, I can see 'em."

"Shut the hell up, Carl!" Billy snapped, and then glared at Norris. "And what dah hell do yuh tink you're gonna do wit dem? Tink yuh gonna take all five of us on, asshole?"

"He's a pile of shit, Billy," the dark haired stocky middle pimp grumped. "He ain't gonna do shit. But just to show 'em dat he really is a total asshole, let's change his pretty face for him."

Billy's nodding grin brought forth another indict-ment. "And wit dat flat top haircut, he's eder queer or some rich punk from out in Hamilton or Parkdale. Dey all deserve ah going over."

"You heard 'em. You queer? "Street shifted his weight slightly to his right and brought each bottle out to rest on his thighs.

"Yeah, Carl. He is a dumb ass asshole. And if yuh really don't want to spend ah couple of weeks in the hospital, put dem bottles down and fight fair!" Street almost laughed at the paradox.

"Five of you … One of me … Fair?!"

"Listen asshole…yuh try using one of dem and we're really gonna do ah number on yuh face! You got dat?"

"And Billy Boy, the first one of you gets one of these in his face and the second what's left that cuts deep, and then we'll see where this goes from there."

Norris' tone was void of emotion, even tone, just like the Marine Hand to Hand Combat Instructor demanded was the only way to neutralize aggression. As he spoke he brought his right hand slightly up and forward and as the street light reflected from its thick base he added in that same deadness, "So who's first?"

Billy and Carl began to bounce, both hands up and clenched. The Redhead put his right hand in his pocket but left it there. Street's focus was on his chosen target.' Shorty's' expression was as steady and focused as his balance. He shifted that as his eyes never left Street. But Norris knew Shorty would not be the first one up. That would always be the Bottom Bloke...the one who was the brunt of crude jokes and insinuations questioning his manhood. *The Bottom of the Totem Pole* as the Combat Instructor labeled them. The one whose status demanded he prove his peer's judgments wrong. *It never is, but that's why the beggar's always got to go first*, the short always grinning British Commando leading their hand to hand combat instruction had added. So the Sacrificial Lamb was the medium-sized, pimple pocked marked cheeked one to the right of the center pin.

Street was concentrating too deeply on the slow ballet each of his five targets began, so he really didn't understand why the Center Point and The Lamb had jumped. Or why they didn't come down. The last question forced him to take a quick, peek above their heads, as if they were suspended on a wire. That was outrageous. And so were two of the other three bullies suddenly turning then scurrying and finally the small wake and shower of sparks their steel cleat heels created on the rough cobbled stones. It was only then that Norris noticed the suspended pair was being held about six inches in the air by another human.

"So, what you want got in mind for dese two Boss?" The overly deep basso chuckle forced Street to shift at least his visual attention back to the two suspended duck tails held aloft by a black male whose dimensions were so outrageous the duck tails seemed like Christmas ornaments attached to a tree. He seemed to exert the least effort but both ornaments were extremely involved. He also noticed the dangerous one had not turned and fled. Instead he gave the huge Black a careful optical going over shrugged, then walked up the block until he vanished around a corner.

"I guess that one didn't want nuttin' to do with either you or me..." There was a long pause as Street took in the insanity two grown men suspended...It was too insane.

"So what you want me to do with dese two bozos, Boss?" When Street told him to let them go, they both hit the cobblestones running and didn't pause until they vanished into the semi-muggy dark.

For a few seconds Street simply gawked in wonder over the ebony giant with his muscles chiseled in the style of Michelangelo's David who remained, feet spread almost as wide as the impish smile. The biceps were so large he had to cut the sleeves from his Tshirt. Even so it still looked like his shoulder muscles would split it any instant if he moved too quickly. He was easily four inches taller than Street's six feet two and had a waist which challenged his own thirty inch girth. In the end he guessed his savior had to wear a hat near a size nine, though Street had never seen anything that large.

"Thanks."

"From here it didn't looked like you needed too much help. I thought you had 'em buffaloed, boss."

"One of 'em was about to make a big mistake and...no matter what, I was going to see an emergency room before it was done." As Street tried to think of some more words to show how grateful he was, the beast took a couple of steps and confronted him almost nose to nose, even though Street was standing on the curb. Up close its physique rendered him speechless for a full three inhalations as he assessed it.

"Glad I could help."

After a short bit of chuckling, Street learned his name was Rodney and he worked at Sparrows Point Steel Mill. He had a wife and two kids who he was demanding, "Go to college if I got ah bust their collective butts five times a day!"

Rodney had been one of the sixteen million along with Street to fight *The Good War*. "But all I was, was a Black butler for a racist colonel. Never even got to go to the rifle range! I guess they was scared about letting us Black Boys get guns in our hands."

All of this was gleamed while they waited for the bus. They took the first set of seats behind the middle door since this was as far forward as Rodney's race was allowed, even if the bus or street car was entirely empty. Rodney had to turn toward the window so Street could fit in without blocking the aisle with his shoulder. They both ignored the puzzled stares by later Black boarders. Street got off at Harford road and waved after Rodney said he'd see him again.

Monday night Rodney gushed about 'How good my kids is doing in school' and how he had just made a down payment on a row house. "It's on the White Side of North Avenue,' he offered with his beaming row of perfect white teeth. Street praised him and added that he was planning to marry during the Christmas holidays but he deleted his military service.

For the rest of the week they talked sports, a bit of local politics and some general bitching about their jobs. He discovered Rodney was the Number Two Helper at an open hearth furnace and made good money. He knew what an open hearth was but he hadn't a clue what the duties of a Number Two Helper entailed.

So it went and the following Monday when Rodney didn't show up for the last bus Street surmised he was on vacation. In two weeks he began to wonder if that was correct, so Tuesday after he didn't show, Street walked to the very rear of the bus and asked the five occupants on the last seat if they knew Rodney. All but one nodded.

"Is he still on vacation?"

"Man we don't get no vacation unless we get burned." In the short quiet space between that declaration Street felt his breath cease for three heart beats.

"We hope he's on vacation forever," the oldest looking replied. Street didn't like the tone."

"Sorry, man, I don't get you."

"He dead," A really long thin and light skinned male in a coal dust stained Tshirt offered."

"He got killed...Dah plug broke too … Number Two's break dah cement plug wit a steel rod. Got ah be careful, get outta the way or…" Street never heard all the rest of the details. They went through his brain never stopping to take root. When the narration ended he asked if anyone knew Rodney's home address. No one did, or if he had a telephone—and worst of all, none of them knew his last name! So, there was no way to check to see if he had a phone.

It seemed the Cross Town bus took over an hour to cover what was normally a twenty minute run. Habit led him to their seat. He as the only Caucasian staring out the open window and waiting for the Sears store window to appear and signal he wanted off long enough to stop him from remembering two terrified young men suspended in midair, held aloft by invisible dark energy.

Once he got off he decided the three mile walk to Halcyon Avenue wasn't that long. It turned out to be just long enough for him to stop muttering and wiping away tears, but not allow him to dismount from Rodney's image.

Next morning Street called Sparrows Point and when he finally got connected to the personal office, he was politely informed they would not confirm if Rodney worked there…had been injured or killed…unless he had a last name. Then he checked the *Baltimore Morning* and Evening Sun Papers and when they told him they had no such record. When he revealed Rodney's race he was told less politely, but with a civil tone that neither edition listed Black Deaths.

Finally he called the Afro-American and after giving his scanty information was told to call back in two days. When he did someone growled that they didn't hold death records after three days. Then he turned to real estate agents to see if they could tell him where a Black could buy a home on the North side of North Avenue and was either laughed at for asking that impossibility… then, got a click as the line died.

So he persisted and started walking the areas he thought Rodney's house could be. Middle September was still pouring its excessive heat and humidity on still un-air conditioned, lower middle class Baltimore. In his search he did discover that any Black influx was only five blocks from end to end…all sixty year old row houses with twenty nine to each block.

Most of his knocking and door bell ringing was not acknowledged. However, he was certain faces were peering through the heavy laced curtains. Finally a door opened and an overly tall, thin, light skinned lady framed it. She not only told him she could not help him with his search, she added in a hush, "Folks around here don't want none of your kind nosing round.

So don't ask no questions. You better skedaddle before a couple guys take you in an alley."

He finished his canvas anyway. No one opened a second door.

"Damn it Rodney. I know you lived. You weren't some god damned figment of my imagination …" he stopped when he realized he was speaking aloud and everyone back of the middle door was not only listening but shaking their heads. So, he finished it silently… How the hell could a man your size, with your zest for life just vanish into … when he could not construct any medium which could swallow Rodney? He stepped off the bus and Rodney's projection slowly faded into history. But it was another ten years before he no longer had a need to answer that last question.


## Part Three: Intermezzo

The latest completed section of Interstate I-95 between Baltimore and Washington DC supported three lanes of traffic moving along ten miles an hour faster than the 55 MPH posting in both directions. Street was thinking about his lesson plans for his four senior economic classes and basking in the wind whipping about his face. He had the top down on his brand new Fiat 124 red convertible obeying the speed limit and all was good with the world. At least for the morning of this present one.

"Maybe that's too optimistic," he addressed the dash. Silently the fuel gage agreed with him. It was obvious to even him that the only thing good in 1974 was the grade of dope one smoked. He was trying to think of some way to make *The Economies and Diseconomies of Scale* relevant. Relevant was the golden treasure word for this drugged out bunch.

"Hey Mister N, man, Is this really relevant with what's going down?" He was about to reply aloud that he really didn't give a rat's ass and that everything he did in class would be on the final exam when a four door cheery red Cadillac pulled ahead of him and inch by inch forced him onto the apron and then to a stop

Three of the Caddy's doors opened and three large males piled out making a mad dash back to him as Norris frantically reached under his seat searching blindly for the tire iron. As his fingers found nothing two hands fastened on his sport coat collar and a husky heavily accented baritone screamed, "Out! Jesus! Get out! Now! It's ready to blow, man!

The human vise grips pulled him backwards until he was sitting on the seat's top "Get the hell outta there! Run! Run for it!" The tone was so honest, so laced with both terror and concern for his welfare, all Street could do was obey.

He rolled off the seat's back and followed the trio as they raced up the high, almost bare of grass bank but scattered with thorn bushes bordering the apron. Thorns and stickers tore at his legs but he never paused until he joined the three of them perched on the very crest about forty feet above his car and at least fifty yards behind it. When he looked down his heart almost skipped a couple of beats. No one had to point out that his muffler was cherry hot … throbbing cherry hot.

"Holly Hell! It's right under the gas tank!" Street screamed as groups of oblivious commuters ripped by his death-trap; a few going fast enough to shake the Fiat as they passed.

"Si Si!" the owner of the vise grips replied and the accompanying duo nodded, with the tallest pointing just to be sure the gringo understood what was going to happen if he went much further. *I'd end up as a damn Roman candle,* Street thought.

"Halba español, Señor?"

"Español del calle, solamente."

"Only the Spanish of the streets? This is good! It means you are a traveler not a touristo," Vise Grips offered. Even though his speech was deeply etched with either a Mexican or Central American accent the smile was one of acceptance…not humorous. Street was about to thank them all, when the short, totally bald but full bearded one held out an unlabeled clear pint bottle which was half-filled with a pale amber liquid.

"It's really good hooch," Vise Grips explained as Street almost pulled back from the invitation. With a slight shrug and smile he accepted it, uncapped and took a very short snort. It was good hooch. So he had another longer one to the verbal approval of the entire trio.

When he passed it back to Baldy, he really took a good look at his saviors. He had never seen a deeper black complexion. He surmised they were from along the coastal region of wherever they hailed from since the Spanish had forced the freed Black slaves to live there because of the oppressive heat, humidity, man eating crocs and poison infected snakes. The third silent one was perhaps a tone darker and the tallest; almost as tall as Norris.

"We're all un-documented. Got jobs at Fort Meade on a sub-contracting job." Vise Grips nodded to his companions. "Juan's from Nicaragua. Jose and me are Honduran. You been to either of those?"

Street nodded. "Yeah Copan and … But look, I'm indebted to you guys for the rest of my life." They all laughed when he added, "For my life."

"May it be long and may you have many beautiful women join your bed."

"What's your name? "

"Javier. My Father and his Father was Javier back to the chains the Spanish locked around them when they came over from Nigeria."

"I … Look, I want to thank you more than …"

"Of course but is already done. Your eyes show we are not your saviors, Senor … we are your equals … and that is much more important … no?" Street nodded even if he didn't really understand or agree. However, he did not reach in his pocket for his wallet.

"So we are late to work. Will you be so kind to take this phone number and call our jefe and tell him why?" That brought a long burst of chuckles and Baldy slapped him on a shoulder. He agreed and after another snort they started back to their car. Only then did Street Norris realize he had to know why they stopped and why hundreds of other passing cars had not. So he ran up as they were opening the doors.

"Javier Why the hell did you guys decide to stop?" Vise Grips turned, ran a hand over his tightly curled dreadlocks and shook his head very slowly.

"I guess it is weird for you … Three Black monsters piling out and coming at you to save your life … It was not so for us … We saw the heat and Juan and Jose yelled for me to get you off the road … I was already pushing at you by then." He looked up at the full sun and nodded. "I guess it's because when you see someone in trouble and when you love life as much as we do, you have to pull over and see if you can help."

There was another long pause until Jose interrupted. "And what is your name?"

"Street, and before I forget, can I have your telephone number and address so I can get in touch later?"

As Javier nodded and wrote them on the back of a check out list he added, "No wonder you speak the Spanish of the Streets!" That got a chuckle. "You may have been to our countries but you can never know how wonderful it is to be here! How we love sending money home to help our mothers. How we wake up every morning with smiles as big as the room we share. So, that maybe is another reason why we stopped to help you, Street."

That shut off all other questions. He nodded. Then they got in and pulled off. Street drove only as far as the nearest filling station, where he called their boss, and also one of his own colleagues whom he asked to come and pick him up, all in that order. Not because he was afraid the car would explode … but because he could not tolerate the images of the Black kids playing football … or Rodney's grin when they met at the bus stop … and last but not any less demanding, the understanding softness some vise grips had. He sat waiting for his friend, Vise Grips' words echoing in his head … *when you love life as much as we do.*

Maybe it's time to start loving my own life, Street thought. Or maybe he said it out loud.

# Satan ... A Dog's Story

"Look if you want my advice say good bye to him out here. Don't go in when I put him to sleep. I can't stress that too strongly." Kurt Jefferies shook his head but contained his thoughts. *Don't tell me what I should and shouldn't do! Ten years ago you were a senior in my Humanities class! You got no right to tell me anything! Your rights are still the same. You got the right to shut up, sit down, mind your own business, take good notes and ask intelligent questions.*

"I'm going in, Bobby," Doctor of Veterinary Medicine Robert F. Clancy's grimaced.

"Well, wait a bit. There's no hurry and I ... "

"Why? He ain't going to get any better. And ..."

"He's not in any pain, Doctor Jefferies." Clancy's conferring his academic credentials was also accompanied by a strong hint of professional distain.

"Yeah Bobby, but this is what I want to do.

"Very well if you really insist," Clancy was half turned before he added; "My nurse will let you know when I'm ready." Before Jefferies could reply he shoved the swinging doors and vanished.

Jefferies looked down at the patient and whispered, "Why does he want to prolong this?" Then he faced the door and spoke loudly enough so the teen age receptionist heard. "What the hell! All you use is a needle Bobby. So come on and stop being a pouting jerk." The short Hispanic desk clerk was up and followed Clancy leaving Kurt face to face with Satan.

His long black fluffy coat still held a few feeble ripples of gleaming robustness and his length could still awe a casual observer; or terrify any off-hand threat. The enormous head and massive jaws still housed chalk white fangs and molars which could still command not only respect but also stinging fear. The legs looked strong enough to lift him over a six foot fence with daylight to spare. And all these qualities were instantly erased by his emaciated bulk.

Slowly Jefferies squatted and laid a palm on that wondrously huge head. "Couple of months ago you still hit a hundred and a half on the scales. Now you ain't sixty-five. Sixty-three and three quarters to be precise." His tone was half a growl and when Satan tried to lift his head, Jefferies slid his palm under it and raised it enough so he could press his lips to the cold wet nose.

"Love you," he whispered into the thick fur covering the muzzle. "Damn it. I've loved you since I got you when you weren't even a dozen weeks old. All ears and paws. And a tail that looked like it belonged on a rat. Loved you since … Since …" His voice cracked completely so he finished the last part silently. Later he admitted to the mirror on the far wall that he had said something he had managed avoiding his entire life.

*"Maybe you're the only other living thing … the only … Oh God What if you and Lois are the only love I've had for any … Ain't that a crock? Wouldn't that really be something? Nope … No … It would be … It wouldn't be so terrible. Hasn't been … I'm really gonna …"*

***

When the almost coal black German Shepherd pup came into his life two months short of twelve years ago, a span which seemed more like three disintegrating fleeing worlds ago, history possessed just two separations; B.C., events before the birth of Christ and A.D., the abbreviation for Amino Domino: events after the birth of Christ. Unconsciously Jefferies later added, B.S. … Before Satan.

"You were just a bundle of fur with oversized ears and your paws were almost the size of tennis rackets. And you were black all over except for these four brown paws. The vet told me not to get use to anything except the size of your ears and paws. That your breed change color, fur texture, but that never happened to you. And the month I had you before I sent you up to those crazy monks in Jersey for basic training, all you did was poop, eat, grow and sleep.

"Okay … yeah … I gotta give it to you. I did use to put you up on my bed. You didn't get up there on your own. But I had a good reason. Up there you couldn't tear up the carpets and chew up my shoes. Okay … don't give me the evil eye … that's all crap. You never chewed anything. So now I'll admit it. It just seemed you really belonged up there with me. You felt good. Good as … and I got to admit you never crapped on it, or peed either.

"The monks were amazed when I told them you only went outside. Didn't tell 'em how you yapped your fool head off until I got awake to take you in the yard. And I never told you I thought you were going to be deformed because your paws were way too large. But every month I had to come to that weird ass place on the Jersey Shore so you could get use to me all over again, they got smaller … Just kidding. You grew into 'em really fast. And you knew me the instant I pulled in. I got you back eight months later. That's when I started thinking I was watching one world after another barge on the scene and then disappear like some bad movie that was hyped and died the first week it hit the Multiplexes.

"Not that any of this mattered to you but there were two nasty shooting wars going on. I could have told Bush to stay outta Afghanistan. How can you expect a bunch of isolated tribes become a nation and use us as a model? Not when from one valley to the next they don't speak the same dialect and never worship Allah the same. I could have told them to get out of a place that has only one paved road and that one was built by the Russians just to get their tanks in there!

"Then there was … You listening to me? Sorry … I didn't mean to raise my voice …Okay … let's forget the crap."

"You know … there for a second I thought you were saying something to me. That's insanity ain't it? I know you got a good vocabulary, and you even know how some of them are spelled. I haven't a clue how big yours is, but dogs don't talk!" He reached over and rubbed the nose again. His reward was a soft licking about his palm. He had to turn aside and wipe the tears coursing down his cheeks. He gave a deep exhale and his head a tiny shake so Satan couldn't see how hurtful this was.

"Gotta admit, once you were grown and we started traveling together I never needed a pick up line as long as I had you with me. You've always been the greatest when it came to that… If you could understand me, I'd really thank you for the entire bevy of good looking stewardess and all the other gorgeous women you sent my way. Not that, What's *a nice person like you doing in a place like this? Or 'Yeah I'd love to go out with you but first I think I have to tell you that I have an iron clad rule. I never … well seldom kiss on a first date,'* didn't work.

"Anyway let's thank KLM and BOA for letting a pet ride in a seat if it's in First Class! First time I took you up that tall blonde, Janet? Soon as we got into the seat belts she was back there squatting right by you."

Suddenly Jefferies had to resist reaching over, picking Satan up and walking out because of the way the dog was gazing at him; as if it was trying to tell him all the wondrous times they had had weren't enough. He somehow sensed Satan was trying to tell him that he wanted their relationship to go on and on, like the universe.

"Hey Dude! Where'd you get the idea you could out live me? You ain't … "He paused and ran his fingers along the torso, trying to demand they tell him how he could create a cure. There was hardly any meat between the thick hairy coat and the ribs. He ended with some gentle pats.

"What do women see in dogs anyway? The second Lois saw you she was in love.

"Remember when you were still a year old pup, Lois and I took you to that Mexican beach where the hotel owner had his own little zoo? Doves and rabbits and a dozen or so cats, five parrots and every one of them had a name?

"Maybe you don't remember them but I bet you never forgot *The Pack*; those five Mongrels and Lobo, the Alpha, half German Shepherd? They surrounded you and whipped your butt good! If I hadn't told La Senora to call them off you'd have gotten a thrashing every morning. Lois was really pissed about them ganging up on you. I thought she was gonna take 'em on. And she would have, you know? She really loved you … me too."

That thought made Jefferies pause. After some pats and rubs he managed to separate the two as Satan's posture seemed more alert. His eyes were definitely brighter and one paw now rubbed Jefferies' hand.

"I'm positive we went back there two years later so she could see you were up to them." He grasped the extended paw. It still smothered his palm.

"And you beat the snot out of each and every one. We came in and they were waiting for you just inside the veranda like it was *West Side Story* and they were *The Sharks?* I still see 'em coming out and surrounding you. and two minutes later they're all hiding in the kitchen. Nope … you really had it in for Lobo! You chased his butt all the way out on the beach. But that was only after Lois told you to let go of his throat and let him up. And from then on every time he saw you he lit out with his tail between his legs. That was very cool." There were some more light rubs answered by a light kiss on Kurt's eyebrow.

"And from them on for the whole two weeks you ruled the roost:" He gently rubbed an ear. Satan, King of the Pie and Surrounding Areas. When Jefferies regained control he shifted back to history.'

Pausing allowed his visual memory movie to drop him back on that same beach. The three of them were sitting side by side watching a sunset where the sun hissed as it dipped into the ocean and later the emerging stars swarmed in the bottomless dark.

Since their first collision Lois had always been surrounded by children. Crowds of them clustered about her as she taught a group of urchin Peruvian girls to weave string bracelets they could sell to the tourists. Another ten of them in Columbia, their multi colored shredded shawls and skirts reminding him of a wilting floral bouquet.

And on that beach as well as hovering on the outskirts of the human halo in The Andes was when he understood that there were waves beyond his horizon of knowledge, out there where the whales escorted their helpless offspring in the endless black compassion generates. And all three of them, understanding at last, that was where they were meant to be—forever.

He shook and some of his tears disappeared into Satan's coat, as he desperately searched for anything to shatter these images and revelations.

"There was the second war going on when I got you. The one with bunches of long haired crazed idiots running around liberating water fountains and shouting they were going to change the world. Well they have. But not like they wanted to back in 1977, three years before your first year on the job down in Mexico and my flower Co-op.

"Remember when we were at The Pie the last time you charged out growling at the guy who owned the bar? You better! I look up and he's pointing a Luger at you, and I jump off a ten foot sea wall and … I'm facing this jerk and may get shot over a dog! I thought I was out of my skull!" Jefferies reached over and scratched Satan's nose. "You always like getting this. One thing you can't do yourself can you? But there's not much else you can't do is there?

"You know I keep telling everyone you understand everything I say. There's some words like out and back yard I can't even spell without you barking! And that's another thing. You never had a good deep male bark. It sounds like you're still a puppy. But then you never bark or growl when there's real trouble. So I can forgive you about the bark. About … don't make me cry.

"But you and me had important things ahead of us, so I didn't tell you. Didn't want you sitting around and worrying if the whole planet was going to go up in smoke or end up a festering out-house. It was weird that you were there to protect me. That took some getting used to. Like you were really the biggest Colt Forty-five I ever saw."

Now Jefferies sat down and pulled Satan's head on his lap and when there was this deep lingering sigh, he placed his hand so his fingers gently rubbed the long thick snout and caressed folded ears. He ceased speaking and stared about the waiting room as he tried to think of something to stop the pain and tears.

That proved to be impossible so he tried a new line." So you were always the greatest pick up line until Lois came along.

"The undertaker really had a fit when I brought you along. But his wife said it was okay. Said you were too handsome to be a bad dog. But even she didn't want you staying by the coffin all night. So I had to stay too … Thanks. Gave me enough time and privacy so I could tell Lois … try to explain some of my screw ups and … Okay … ask her to forgive me squandering our time together." The head's weight forced Jefferies to shift it slightly, but still keep it on his thighs.

"Both nights I wake up and you're sitting up right below her head. I thought you were on guard … but you know what? It's crazy but now that I look back … I thought lots of times that you honestly believed she'd wake up and need you. There's another thing that I like about you. I use to assume it was a small one, but now I'm an old fool I can see it was large … really large. It tells me how much you loved her and me.

"She always let you lose for your night walks and when I was home and went along, she made me let you go too. Pretty soon I told her about you always disappearing in the shadows or along the edges of our woods. She said you did it the very first time she let you go. Lois said she knew you'd come back if she called so she gave you your head.

"So we took it for granted. Didn't know you were out of sight so you could protect us if anyone tried something funny, like mugging. You could come out of the dark like a devil dog. Hey, that's funny! I didn't realize that until after that night in Guatemala."

They were alone. He surmised this was a special area, but when he glanced up there wasn't a sign reading EUTHANASIA WAITING ROOM anywhere on the three white metal walls or hanging from the center pane on the fourth glass one. Even the paint could not hide the dimples or the small black pock marks where a nail or thumb tack had been driven in to hold as announcement or set of rules. "How can there be rules when you are getting ready to …" Jefferies asked the three green upholstered chairs. The last one on his right nodded its agreement.

Their first real assignment was in the Guatemalan Highlands. Both Jefferies and the dog didn't mind the cold nights and cool days. But Satan did resist riding in a straddling position with his fore and hind legs resting on opposite side of the horse in a canvas sling Kurt had had made for him. This was the first time Jefferies could remember speaking to him as though he was a partner. As a human who could actually understand his monologues. The first time he refused to climb up after the horse was hobbled and stretched out; Jefferies simply told Satan that he could not run freely in the jungle because there were at least ten poisonous snakes and countless deadly insects.

This was also Jefferies' first contact with Ivan Naylor Sane, a short slender Texan who claimed he had been assigned as further protection. Sane had eyes as dark as gun bores and just as frightening when they stared at you. Jefferies decided they were the perfect complement to his blue black hair. He didn't like it that Sane hardly ever spoke above a whisper, a guttural hoarse one at that.

When Kurt pressed the issue why him, Sane confessed he held a sixth degree Karate Black Belt. He did tell Jefferies the first time they stopped for a cup of coffee beside the narrow ancient trail, "I like to sign my name I. N. Sane."

*Just insane is better*, Kurt mused to the vines crawling up to smother the nearby trees.

However, two days later he had no lingering doubts about Sane's qualifications as a body guard. Ivan was confronted by a couple of drunken Germans in a bus station restaurant. They were very drunk and belligerent. Kurt tried to dissuade them but when the larger one persisted and drew back a large worn out looking fist, Sane took about ten seconds to break that one's arm and render the second unconscious and bleeding heavily from both his nose, mouth and left cheek.

They had been returning from moving along the ridge of the central mountain chain that formed the spine of Central America for over a month, stopping in the larger villages which harbored myriad handicrafts. If the village wove blankets, made pottery or shawls, they tried to interrupt the usual process of the police or federal marshals coming in every month or so and buying these products for next to nothing. Which they then took them to the capitol or major tourist centers and sold them for huge profits. It was Jefferies' job to break the endless poverty by forming and financing cooperatives.

He had been at this for nearly fifteen years but up until a year ago he had never encountered any threat to his health or life. But last year, after he got a Co-op going in the capitol with a group of women who made beautiful bead bracelets, the police showed up at his hotel and arrested him

They handcuffed him and took him to the central station, shoved him into a shaky wooden chair and left him. About an hour later a short dumpy guy wearing an officer's epaulettes came in with two squat guards. The officer spoke excellent English elaborately boasting how he had acquired his language skills attending numerous series of CIA clinics on how to deal with gringos who were trying to disturb the stability of Central America. Then he picked up a rubber mallet and hit Kurt on his left cheek hard enough to dislodge three molars and send him sprawling to the damp concrete floor.

When he was asked how he liked that, Jefferies spat the remaining bits of enamel, rolled over so he could stare his tormentor eye to eye and told him, "For a little guy you pack a pretty good punch." That got a sardonic grin, a nod of the head and some comment about for being a stupid gringo he was either a brave man or a complete fool.

Then the officer motioned and muttered something to the duo who picked Kurt up, half dragged him down a long dimly lit hall, undid his handcuffs, opened the green steel door and threw him out into the bright sunlight with enough force to send him sprawling again.

He lay there long enough to thank the Mayan gods lurking on the nearby mountain caps that he was still alive. It was very obvious they had every intention of killing him. As he tried to roll over he thought they would do that to the next one of his group they got their hands on.

Kurt had a difficult time getting over on his back. Once there he was staring up at an attractive face that matched a dark complexion. She was leaning down as she let out a very good scream when she saw his swollen cheek and the dried blood. It got more intense when he managed to sit up and spit a mouthful of it into the gutter.

She got over her fright, helped him to his feet and led him across the street to her pension. *The Good Samaritan* called a doctor who refused to treat him when Kurt explained what had caused his wounds. But Inga Voss turned out to be a lifesaver as well as a good looking Dutch lady. Once the doctor left she got some towels and aspirin. It took a lot of effort to clean him up as well as quite a few aspirins to quell some of the shooting pain. Then she told him to go out to the airport, find KLM and tell them to take him wherever they were going. And when he told her the police had kept all his money and passport she shrugged and said it didn't matter. That all he had to do was show them his face and they would fly him out. "They are Dutch. We are good people. They will help you." He never forgot those eleven words.

He spent a full day in Dallas getting his broken jaw and fractured cheek bone repaired. After he flew back to Washington and met with Barrington Trust's Board of Directors they decided that in the future he would have a guard dog and pick up a weapon once he was in country. As almost an afterthought it was also decided there would also be a human bodyguard for certain assignments. Once he got to know and trust Sane, he always hoped they would become a constant team. That wasn't to be.

Satan spotted the first five corpses the afternoon after Jefferies had established a weaver's Co-op in San Juan de la Alta, an ideal mountain village. The dog caught the scent of death and gave a very deep growl as he managed to get free from his sling. Sane turned his mount and followed. He pulled up a few yards off the trail and bent over. When Kurt rode up Satan was sniffing the mature male body. Neither dismounted immediately. Sane took the path and rode along it until it bent sharply. When he was certain no one was about, he came back and waited until Jefferies came out of the dense strand of stunted pines, dismounted and dropped beside the dog.

Sane said he'd found two other bodies half buried beneath fresh pine branches. So, Kurt got up and followed him on foot to the others. After he pulled some of the branches off, he saw that the blood from the two wounds on each body was still damp. Even so a small battalion of vicious red ants was already at work. Kurt was about to get closer when Satan silently half crouched, his tail dropped between his legs. Jefferies ordered the dog not to move as Sane got his weapon from under his bed roll, slipped out of the saddle, and crouched behind the horse for some semblance of cover.

Kurt scanned the area while Sane called out in Spanish for the person to come out or they would begin shooting. When there was no response Kurt nodded to Satan who bent low as he disappeared into the underbrush. They followed. In about ten yards they met the dog standing guard over two naked adolescent girls, cringing behind a clump of dried weeds. Since Sane's Spanish was impeccable he began asking them the standard questions while Kurt went back to his horse and dug out a couple of tee shirts from his pack. He came back and tossed one to each.

After they squirmed into them, Sane pulled Jefferies off to the side while Satan stayed at attention. He said it was obvious they'd been raped. They had also told him where their three brother's bodies had been dumped. Kurt gave Satan the search command and in less than ten seconds his soft bark announced his discovery.

When Sane got there, Kurt was bent over the largest of the trio, but after a moment or so he gave up trying to drive away the flies walking on the shrunken eyeballs. He was startled when Sane shot one of the ravens trying to yank a meal from the protruding tongue of the one just off the trail.

Since they had to use branches it took a couple of hours to dig all the graves. It would take much longer for Kurt to forget the odors of exposed entrails and the crystal consistency of dried blood puddles. On the way to the girl's village they had to stop again and bury an elderly woman prone among her half-finished wash beside the first ford their horses had to wade.

Once in the village they could really focus on the girls. The oldest claimed to be eleven and her sister nine as she led them down the path to a cluster of dented sagging log huts in various stages of rot. Sane rode off as Kurt tried to comfort the grandparents. He wasn't back at dusk. Jefferies unrolled his sleeping bag and Satan dropped at his feet. He was so exhausted he only raised his head long enough to see his canine guard on all fours but the huge head erect and motionless.

Sane was sleeping across from him when he opened his eyes. Satan stretched out as soon as Kurt sat up and was asleep in the middle of a deep sigh. He crawled out, gave his buddy a couple of rubs behind his flattened ears, ignoring the slight protesting grunt and decided not to wake his companion until he had some breakfast ready.

But before he started coffee he noticed Sane's carbine resting beside him. When he retrieved it so he could wipe the dew from the barrel, he ejected the thirty round clip and checked its contents. There were only nine rounds. He immediately decided not to ask any questions as to why. Sane wasn't at all timid discussing his deed once he was awake and had two cups of black coffee. He did it in exactly fifty words, delivered with as much emotion a normal person would use to describe putting out the weekly trash.

"Got the first four one at a time. That left two. No guns just machetes … sleeping. At first I was gonna shoot them but I still see the girls. I hit 'em on the head … staked 'em out. Cut their foreheads and calves. Made sure the ants found 'em."

After forming three more Co-ops without any further bloodshed or intimation, they were back in the capital, in the same bar where Sane had destroyed the German sailors before he asked, "Whatever got a nice guy like you into something this dangerous?"

Kurt had to admit he had been wondering why Sane hadn't asked a lot sooner. He gave him a very brief, sketchy and almost completely untrue answer. But later in Miami when sleep would not come, he rose, stared out the window and began telling the sky with its blood red clouds. Actually his thoughts were directed more to the huge pink roses that formed and dissolved in some of their parents' centers.

***

Kurt Wolfgang Jefferies' biography prior to joining Barrington Trust had been a hodge-podge of snap decisions beginning with his underage enlistment in the Navy, plus a later off-hand choice for a university where he could chase more sophisticated ladies. The worst was deciding to spend five years with General Motors after graduating with a master's degree in economics. He managed to get fired half-a -year after he became the second youngest manager in that closed society's history.

He had an American Fox Hound named Spotty and a steady named Gertrude who managed refreshments at the local Waco Texas AMC Cineplex. After his dismissal he was forced to move back to Baltimore and he left Spotty to her nine year old son. Later he liked to claim, *It was a marriage made in buttered popcorn.*

His finances were so depleted he took the first job which hired him without delving into his background; a long term substitute at a local high school. And since the system only paid twice a month and he refused to eat canned beans for a full fortnight, he took a part time position as a Limo driver.

His fourth client was Bradford Douglas Barrington. The only words he exchanged with his client were, "Yes sir, No sir" and a heartfelt "Thank you sir" when B.D., as he requested to be addressed, handed him a fifty dollar tip.

In the next two weeks B.D. used him on a nightly as well and full weekend basis. In that time Kurt decided he could not tolerate servitude and that he also loved teaching. So the day he got his first paycheck and decided he could survive, he tended his resignation to *Exclusive Limos Limited*. The next afternoon B.D.'s administrative assistant phoned. She asked if he was interested in chauffeuring B.D. on the weekends. He really wasn't but a hundred and twenty-five a day guaranteed was a sufficient enticement.

When the school term ended, he applied for a full time position as an economic and humanities provisional instructor and was hired. Later he discovered it was his math minor which got him the job. And since his first paycheck wouldn't arrive until the last day of September, B.D. became a six day a week, sixteen hours a day gig which for the summer only, included a nicely furnished room over the five car garage and three better than average meals each day. Over the following ten weeks he was engrossed in B.D.'s routines and gained access to a small part of his accompanying mysteries.

B.D. didn't work, had never worked. Unless one thought supervising three full time gardeners' constant efforts at providing an ever changing colorful backdrop for his glass enclosed swimming pool, patio, and hot tub complex. His obvious horticulture obsession was his prize winning boxwoods.

He also spent a few hours each day selecting and maintaining the eighty medical students he supported through their seven to ten years of medical education. Kurt soon discovered his summer boss made all his selections based solely on intelligence and poverty levels for each one. And he also did not sexually discriminate even though female doctors were still somewhat of a rarity when he began this in the middle fifties.

The remainder of his day was devoted to social networking on a purely face to face basis, with a concentration on the affluent Washington, Annapolis, Baltimore suburbs. This was Kurt's busy time, chauffeuring from riverside mansion to just a mansion or from horse estate to house estate.

B.D. never used the limo on these forgings. So Jefferies spent endless hours reading and listening to classical music in any of five cars. He liked the 1927 Rolls' perfumed soft calfskin back seats best. However, the 1940 Mercedes was almost as nice. The gems of the convoy, the 1959 Aston Martin and the 37 Jag convertible were only used for Georgetown excursions. Usually the 29 Packard sixteen cylinder town car only nosed into Baltimore's hollowed Gilford division. Kurt despised this one because his seat was open to the early morning dew or oppressive humidity. However, it was never used if there was the slightest hint of any type of precipitation. Two days before the Fall Term began, Jefferies made his final most lasting decision and it was a snap one … just like his decision to become an educator and later a husband.

It was early afternoon when his house phone rang and Helmet, the estate overseer, announced that B.D. would like him to come to the library in half-an-hour. This piqued his interest. In his nine weeks the only two rooms he had been privy to were the staff's dining room and the humongous kitchen.

"Come in."

No first name, no mister, not even an ounce of superiority.

"Have a seat and can I fix you anything?" Kurt gesture was negative as he was motioned to a brown leather chair opposite his employer.

"Before I make you my proposition I better fill you in. Okay? And are you certain I can't fix you something?"

Kurt passed again.

"By the way this isn't a shot at you becoming my permanent chauffeur, Kurt."

The narrative lasted well over an hour and began in London being discharged from the Army Air force late 1945. Instead of fleeing back across the Atlantic, he decided to give Paris a go. The Paris of 1946-47 wasn't the artistic magnet it had been after *The War to End All Wars*. But it was still Paris and he devoured its charms, vices, elegant life style and humanitarianism. The last led to three years traversing Southern Africa, India and Central America.

"Kurt, this is the first time I got up close to people whose future was servitude, struggle and eventual starvation or death by disease. It really pissed me off. Nope. It made me guilty at being so lucky. I didn't have a clue at just how terrible *The Great Depression* had been. I wasn't even aware there had been one."

He gave a sardonic grin before adding, "Dad wouldn't let me read *The Grapes of Wrath* or see the movie either!

"Outside Cape Town I pulled my rental car up to the entrance of a black township and five white, armed to the teeth guards informed me that only white politicians and government employees could gain entrance. You could smell the stink a mile before you saw the rusting barbed wire fences."

He paused, rubbed his two toned van Dyke and added, "But the slum outside Monterey Mexico, the one built out of packing cases and discarded cardboard boxes, was the final straw. Or maybe a nail would be better.

"When I got home it was the upper classes' unconcern that bothered me the most. And I got home just in time for Dad's fatal stroke and two days after we put him the family mausoleum, Mom withdrew to her favorite vacation home in Maine. As she got into our twin engine Cessna, her last words were, *Do whatever you want to with the money, Banny. Just don't let us all end up in the poor house*. Three hundred or so million and change made that as easy request to grant.

"I decided the family wealth was going toward demolishing those packing case houses. Use it to find a way to bring sewage and clean water into living hells like the one I couldn't get into. A year after Dad died, I patented the Jiffy Toilet. We've dispatched nearly two hundred thousand of them and never charged a dime."

He went on that he realized he needed expertise and he made his first huge mistake by seeking government help. He soon learned that the State Department, International Monetary Fund and the International Development Bank were all his silent but very efficient foes. That *The enemy of my enemy is my ally* was the *Golden Rule* for controlling third world governments. "That the only concern our government had been and still is to maintain the status quo politically, economically and socially in developing nations."

This all changed when he stumbled on *The Seventh Day Adventist* worldwide medical program. He found there were no attempts at conversion or missionary efforts. Just a low keyed individualized, even a customized effort to fit the needs of specific areas. So he sent some volunteers to observe and after a couple years he had a plan.

"I started with medical clinics in El Salvador. Brought in free vaccinations and talked six of my college buddies who were doctors, and each had a different specialty, to make the rounds. I had nineteen clinics by then so they went down for three weeks and damned if they didn't recruit another team and before I knew it I had eighteen teams! From then on all I have to do is ship in the medications they ask for. It's truly amazing how deeply humanitarianism can run inside those sacred white jackets.

"A brand new GP, Donald Fleming, gave me the idea of buying a boat and outfitting it into a floating hospital and sail it up and down both coasts. So I bought a tramp steamer, outfitted it and it was so successful that in ten years I bought three more.

One for South America and the other two for Africa and there's a waiting list of volunteers from nurses to brain surgeons.

"However I got the seed for what I'm going to ask you to join from a drunk in Cannes, France. He claimed there was always going to be more and more sick people as long as they don't have enough to eat or buy decent housing and clothes. And if I wanted to really invest my money wisely, use it to change the economic structures this planet's poor has been subjected to for at least the last thousand or so years.

"So we're going into developing hundreds of Co-ops. It gets rid of corruption and for a few thousand dollars it can upgrade an entire village, even a small town. And after a summer with you, I think you're ideally suited. So what do you say?"

Jefferies not only said yes he also nodded as he did.

***

Kurt smiled as he recalled how B.D. deliberately skipped over all the training he was going to undergo. First came SCUBA certification to a depth of fifty meters, a second degree Black Belt in Karate and gaining enough proficiency in Spanish so he could find an interpreter. Also, a physical training regime that took fifteen pounds off his already muscular frame. Then survival training in three phases: The Arctic, Tropical and Wilderness, and each one managed to erode a few more pounds until the reflection in the bedroom mirror reminded him of how he looked when he was playing defensive back in a top college program.

Last was the weapons and demolition sessions and he decided he wasn't going to ask the reason for these when he had been told that his mission was purely a peaceful attempt to alter the economic hell three quarters of the world's population fell into.

***

A couple of weeks after the massacre he and Satan were traversing the central Honduran highlands. He had taken a couple of weeks setting up a weaving Co-Op in San Juan de Valle, a peaceful village set in a deep valley alongside a fairly unpolluted stream. He had also supervised digging three latrines

79

away from it. He was alone now. Sane had gotten sick and had to be pulled out.

San Juan's *jefe* had told him about La Gardena and its famous beautiful blankets woven by a select female group. Female weavers were a fascinating oddity, so Jefferies decided he'd head there. El Jefe hadn't added that it was a three day, straight up track that even Satan protested early each afternoon.

He called it quits when they came upon a rather wide grassy plateau late afternoon. It was his third day and even though he could see and smell the village's smoke he decided he'd like to spend the night out in the open. And he also made up his mind it would be nice to have a fire and create a hot meal rather than using his camp stove to heat up a freeze dried tasteless mess, he called the hot red and white glue according to their respective color.

He was awakened by a fleeting touch across his upturned cheek which made him think he was being attacked by either a scorpion or a snake. His emerging panic resided when he realized it was a paw and Satan was crouched by his side. When the dog's posture indicated aggression his panic was erased by decision making as he half rose and saw why Satan was crouched, head frozen, ready to attack on command.

The trio was similarly attired in shredded serapes and frayed straw sombreros. Each had a short machete half hidden at their sides among the tattered jackets. One slightly taller and a bit more filled out was planted just to the left of the still vigorous fire. The shorter pair was centered behind it. Unconsciously Jefferies right hand fumbled for his weapon while the other reached out to restrain Satan. When it didn't make contact he took a quick glance. The dog was gone.

"Good night senor" the taller one half smirked in the local dialect. "We were wondering if you had some coffee you could spare us." Kurt's eyes swept the area but did not spot Satan.

"Coffee at three in the morning? This café closed hours ago, amigo."

"Some bread then? Perhaps a few dollars?" He moved slightly to his left making sure Kurt saw his weapon. He took only three steps. Not enough to create a semi-circle of fear but enough for Jefferies to spot his canine chaperone. Satan had circled and was crouched directly behind the other two. He was almost invisible in the shadows' edges.

He decided Gary Cooper's poise might discourage this so he let the threat roll off his tongue as if he were telling a bunch of third graders he had caught them stealing his cherries. "No food. No money. And no coffee. But if you want something how's this? I have a gun leveled right on your guts and if any of you take another step I'll shoot. How's that?"

The tall island glanced at his companions. When they gave him no signs he could interrupt he decided to call Jefferies' bluff. While he was in this process Kurt watched his four legged bodyguard slip a few feet nearer the others and crouch even lower so his bulk almost passed as a pile of discarded straw.

"I think you are making a joke. We do not allow guns in Honduras, senor." Still half smiling, Jefferies pulled it free and casually swept the trio. As he watched them draw back a few steps, he realized Satan was no longer crouched behind them. As he pushed his torso more erect he heard a sharp cry of pain shatter the dark behind him. Kurt pivoted just enough so he could see where the next strangled burst came from but he still kept his weapon centered on the frozen trio.

Satan was astride a withering bundle. Kurt pulled himself free from his bag. Once he saw the dog's jaws were locked in the area or the man's neck, he gave the command which allowed some slight easing, yet maintaining contact. Slowly he backed until he was sure the dog's victim was motionless. Then he spun back toward the others, expecting that they would be charging him, machetes raised. Jefferies was alarmed when he realized his brain was ready to accept the need for him to shoot at least one of them. For an instant, as he raised his carbine, he contemplated aiming for a leg.

He confronted only empty night. For an instant he thought the stars were laughing at his predicament like he had once laughed at the silly antics of the Three Stooges films. And then he spun back and trotted over to Satan still straddling the prone motionless figure.

After ordering a complete release he probed the guy's buttocks with the carbine. When he sat up his youth was obvious. "Only a kid," he thought and was about to shoo him off when he noticed the frayed rope with the noose at one end. His finger tightened about the trigger for only an instant.

"Vamoose!" The youngster started to rise but Satan's deep vicious snarl froze him. It almost immobilized Kurt as well. He had never heard such fury come from his guardian's throat. "Down … Good boy …" Now he turned back to the kid and motioned him to get out. He was uncertain getting up accompanied by that same unfamiliar snarl. But once on his feet the kid's speed was startling. In an instant he vanished into the dark.

They both watched him vanish and then he joined Satan in a quick circumnavigation before he threw some more wood on the fire. Then he sat cross legged back to back with the dog and the weapon resting on his legs. After a long stretch of silence and no motion except heavenly ones, he slowly reached behind and stroked the soft fur around the thick neck. Satan moved enough so his head came within his sight range.

"'It looks like we're up for the rest of the night old boy. But, as soon as it gets light, we'll see if we can find the horse and get the hell outta here." He cupped the chin and rubbed. "And by the way thanks. You saved my life. I owe you," and then he laughed. But the dog only stared at him, then let his head swivel so it covered the entire clearing.

When Satan half rose, Kurt recognized the diversion. Honcho their horse sauntered out of the dark, a large bunch of dried grass protruding from his stubby head. "Good to see you know where you next meal is coming from, and where were you when we needed all the help we could get?" He muttered as the horse stopped beside them.

He turned to Satan. "Okay! You win! But being man's best friend doesn't give you more than two cookies." Then Jefferies really laughed, reached over and cupped Satan's full head in both hands. The dark brown eyes were two fixed pin point, centered in that huge but now motionless head. "I love you. And there ain't no cookies right now. But …"

***

"Doctor Jefferies, Doctor Clancy is ready." She paused long enough so it seemed she was trying to remember the rest of a mental note card. He couldn't help noticing that her gaze was centered on the dog and he was obviously an afterthought. And her tone had an aura clearly announcing that he was a bit player, a five dollar ah day extra for this final shoot.

82

"Doctor Clancy still thinks that when you are finished saying good bye it would be best if you waited out here." There was another awkward pause as Jefferies shook his head in disgust and vainly tried not to vent his anger or share his pain. "Doctor Clancy says for you to take just as long as you wish. That he's in no hurry. And he knows how painful this must be."

Ignoring her, Kurt reached over and lifted Satan's head until it rested in his lap again. He bent down so he could stare into those devoted eyes and he didn't give a damn if she saw the tears coursing down both his cheeks. It was obvious Satan's brain was the only part of him still functioning but that was still so strong Kurt was hesitant to start the Last Mile.

"You still got that intensity you know? "He glanced up. Nurse Clara Barton had exited. He simultaneously silently wished she had and hadn't.  He turned back to the eyes. "Remember how your puppy trainer came to me suggesting I set you up for Search and Rescue training because you had such powerful concentration? How he took you out to the obstacle course he used for police dog training and even though you weren't a year old, you did it perfectly after he walked you through it just once telling you exactly what you had to do? "The tail almost managed a weak half wag. He wondered why dogs wagged their tails. Silently he asked the white wall why?

"That was impressive! That's when I started giving you cookies. Yeah maybe I was too impressed. After all, you're still just a … Then when you were a yearling the crazy monks took you again and I had to come up to the Jersey Shore every other weekend and go through all the stuff they were doing to you. Remember that?" He paused, bent over and nuzzled the areas above the eyes. That was answered by a deep sigh, which Jefferies read as a plea for conclusion.

"The one with the beard that came almost down to his waist told me you were the smartest dog he had ever confronted. He also said you were stubborn and for me not to think you were not too bright. Just insist he do his duties.

*He's consumed by that. He'll do his duty even if you don't signal him. We've had a couple like that but never one as bright as Satan. By the way can't you change his name?* And we both laughed.

There was no way I was doing that. The monk gave me a nasty grin and dropped a few more hints. 'His vocabulary already exceeds two hundred words. There are going to be times when you will have to spell out what you are thinking of doing. Or what you don't want him to hear.' How's that for getting a jump on you, buster?" The motionless eyes seemed to mock his sobs the same time they told him how this was helping.

"Lois loved you from the instant you put your head in her lap. Okay, maybe she loved almost any dog. But you weren't a dog to her. Right off she knew how special you were and that something like you only comes along once in a life time.

"Hey! Look at me! You and her had the same relationship she and I had. Yours lasted twice as long. I only had her for five years, three months and nine days. There's never going to be another Lois and never going to be another you, damn it.

"Look at me. Open your eyes. That's it." he reached for the limp ear. "You're boss! Lois bossed me. But you bossed ... "His sobs smothered the conclusion. Even so he was positive Satan understood exactly what he meant.

"You got your weaknesses. *Useless*, that stray kitten Lois brought in from our back yard was one. And yeah Lois was always bringing strays home. And not just animals.

"Anyway, he was just a baby, maybe only a couple days old. I warned her but she insisted you were okay with other animals. It's a damned good thing she wasn't with me that first afternoon I opened the door and you're there with *Useless'* tail hanging out the side of your mouth like a spaghetti straw! I yell and you drop him. He's soaking wet. How long had you been carrying him? I laughed until I cried.

"And he loved you. You'd go to sleep and he'd crawl up between your paws or sneak up so you were his stove. Even when you woke and pushed him away, you never hurt him.

"Well almost never. And I never squealed how every time went out and didn't take you, you met me at the door with Useless hanging out of both sides of your mouth; covered in spit when I made you let him go! She'd have scolded you till you crawled to Hades and back on your belly ... Boy dog."

Jefferies sat, crossed his legs and shifted the head so the eyes pointed toward the wall. Gently he stroked the neck which had once been so thick it had been impossible for him to encircle it with both his ham hock hands. Two mornings ago he had easily slipped them around it. The constant bladder malfunctions and the lack of any real fecal movements had been ignored.

"That's when I knew it was down to this. That the time had … "

They always slept together. When she was still alive Satan jumped on their bed, checked to see they were both snuggled in and then flopped at its foot for a few more minutes. Sometimes he stared at the TV. Lois always liked going to sleep with it on.

"Who did you like most Johnny Carson or Jay Leno? Nope, you were a little too young." He lifted the head and cuddled it closer to his chest. Then he told the wall about another time Satan had saved his life.

"Remember when we were in Ecuador … down on the hot and humid coast … moving from one hell hole to the next? Remember Limones … The rat capital of the world? Rats even crawling up the barnacle covered rotting posts that that crap hole was built on? And you didn't even give them a second glance? And how you scared all the males but the women all laughed when I told them your name was Diablo? How they grinned and joked about petting the Devil?

"And a week or so later right in the middle of when I was trying to set up that farming Co-op in the mountains you started barking like mad while I was trying to talk some of the men into joining up? And when I looked up there's a bunch of soldiers racing toward us? All of them pointing guns and yelling for us to lie down? That we were criminals and they were going to put us in jail? Can you still see that?

"Even though you can run faster, you didn't move until I took off too. And I just figured that out. Thank you. Yeah I know. Don't have to rub it in. If I had followed you we had a good chance of outrunning them. But I took a wrong turn and we ended up at a dead-end on a cliff over a raging river.

"So we're on maybe a fifteen-footer with some really nasty rapids as far as I can see but when I turn to see where you are, you're facing the guns and all. That was really idiotic … Twice over! First I tell you to jump … as if you weren't going to follow me even if I was taking us through the very gates of Hell! You went in like you were in the Olympics trials and I decided to show off … top you and dive like a Tarzan.

"So I dive, not jump. Break all the water safety rules. Never dive in unfamiliar waters. And of course there are rocks everywhere and on the way up I hit one and with the current surging like it was I sort of …

"Okay. Have it your way. I was semi-conscious and if you hadn't grabbed my shirt collar I was gonna drown … maybe. Good thing you got paws as big as tennis rackets and can swim like a Tarzan or I would be …

"And make matters worse when I snap out of it we're zooming through one set of rapids after another but you never let go. It must have been at least half-a-mile before we could get out on that stony beach just above two or three sleeping crocs. And I'm lying on the stones and see that my right arm is broken right above the wrist. That didn't sit too well. Wasn't much chance of running into a doc where we were; was there?

"Two days later I'm half delirious and plodding along behind you. You found water I could drink and even if I couldn't stomach an uncooked whatever you dragged over to me, it was you who got something and you offered it to me first. I'll never forget that. Or that you led me right into a village. How the hell did you know where it was? I guess you smelled 'em … right? When I slipped and fell face down in that stinking goo and couldn't even roll over, let alone get up, you barked enough to bring a couple of half-naked women down who dragged me into a hut.

"But then how did you know a doctor was going to be there? I mean he's making monthly rounds and only there one day every five weeks and he walks up about half an hour after … you're something. I passed out anyway. That was good. I wasn't awake when he set my arm.

"Mister Jefferies the doctor wants to know if you're ready now."

"I'll never be ready. And can't you see I'm half nuts? That I think this dog is talking to me? That he's only the second thing I've ever loved? That he ain't a thing? And neither was Lois. I got poor grades on essays but A's on stories. But this ain't a story. This ain't anything I've ever … I don't give a damn what Bobby says, I'm not ready.

But it was obvious they were both running out of time again and he was once again unsuccessful getting a grip on this mirage called dying.

"Okay." He helped her pick him up and get him on the gurney but he wouldn't allow her to push him through the double swinging doors.

The execution chamber had the same white walls as the reception room and just as austerely furnished. A waist high white metal table covered by a grayish sheet made from some material he could not identify was centered like an altar. There was a shorter tray with oversized wheels against the far wall. The white towel on it wasn't thick enough so he could see the mounds the various instruments created.

The four tube fluorescent ceiling light completed the décor. He was about to make some sarcastic comment about it wasn't a very nice motel for the price he was paying when the other single door squeaked slightly as Doctor Robert Jacob Clancy entered. Jefferies was disappointed that Bobby wasn't wearing a mask to go along with his green smock.

"You really want to do this like this?"

"Yeah, Bobby. This beast means more to me than …"

Bobby, Robert … whomever, shrugged and turned to the tray as Kurt looked around and when he didn't see any other furniture, asked the nurse to get a chair so he could sit. "I want to hold his head while you do it."

There was a long pause as Doctor Clancy shook his head ever so slightly, yet enough so Kurt had to notice and then he motioned to her and she ducked out for a couple of breathes, then came back with a metal folding chair.

So he sat on it and reached over to give Satan's neck a few soft caresses. And when one paw slowly managed to raise itself about half an inch in his direction he grasped it.

Clancy's face slipped between their mutual concentrations. He had a large syringe in one hand and a cotton swap in the other. Kurt gathered Satan's head in his lap. When Clancy lifted the right paw, Jefferies took it, holding it, careful so it did not move when the point disappeared into the thick fur making an initial shallow intrusion.

"This isn't going to hurt," Clancy whispered as he slowly made a deeper insertion. He'll just drop off a few second after I begin so if you want … "

"Shut up Bobby. Just do it."

Kurt felt the neck muscles sag; their full weight slowly fell into his open palm. Then it started forcing his hand lower so he had to strain to keep it from hitting the table top. Satan's head was turned up so Jefferies was staring into the dog's eyes and when the contents of the injection took its total effect they became a pair of polar moons. And then the teeth clamped … popped … then locked tightly. As if Satan had captured a dog's view of mankind and refused to reveal both its secrets and faults.

Casey placed a stethoscope on Satan's silent chest. Kurt thought he was only going through the motions.

"That's it." He rose. "We can take it from here."

"No, Bobby, I'll take it from here. All I want you to do is get him in the back of my car. I'm not as strong as I was when you …"

Clancy had already stepped to the wall phone and was speaking to someone.

He was amazed there wasn't a single objection when he told the crematorium's manager he wanted a dog incinerated. Also there was none when he demanded they keep the furnace door open. But he had it closed as soon as he saw the blue dots and heard the flame's roar enter the chamber. It took longer than he figured, and once again he was almost amused as well as amazed no one objected when he wired the door shut and demanded it stay that way until he paid the bill and returned.

The young blonde male attendant whose flip-flops reminded Kurt of dried blackened snakes let him snap the wire as he handed him a long handled scoop. Jefferies started to place it on the pile but then he shook his head, so the kid did the honors. Kurt thought the pile was much too small to be his dog, but even so it took a while. He had chosen a large urn.

The day was just getting out of bed when he reached Lois' tombstone. It was a brittle sky, slightly laced with thin vaporous clouds that reminded him of egg yolks on a platter. Lois hated eggs. She, too, had chosen cremation, but after her service he insisted on a grave site because he knew he was going to need some place he could come to converse when the music between his ears got to loud.

"Ain't music anymore, darling," he muttered as he sat the urn on the thick grass and settle his butt on her stone. It's just a ringing that keeps getting louder and louder."

He sprinkled some of the ashes and the morning dew absorbed it almost instantly. When it vanished he added more until a slight pile was visible.

"I brought some of him out here. It's just like when he used to crawl up on our bed. And I'm gonna take him with us.

Gonna do the same for him I promised to do for you. Go back and drop some of you both in all the places you loved."

Then the sobs won. They were so strong he almost dropped the urn. As he caught it with his left hand and sat it on the flat thick grass, he added, "Only five years. Just five years. Dear God, that sounds like a long time when you say it. Sounds so ... but now it seems like it was just a long week end."

He half turned but something made him stop and face her again. "I wish it were backwards. You know. Five for him and ...

Suddenly his inner voice smothered his ego and Jefferies sank down beside the marker. "I didn't deserve both of you. I'm ... so grateful. Forever ... finding you two was like being on Iona again. That I should have spent all those years wandering looking for spiritual auras and not haloes. I spent a decade trying to find myself on faded stain glass windows ... damn it.

"Both of you were accidental encounters. Journeys with both of you were always wonderment, enlightening and ... too short. Short because their foundations were always too foreign to digest until later. ... No afterwards ... Unselfish-ness is so alien.

"Lois I didn't know how great you were ... well I knew but it was hard to admit you were even greater than me. When you left instead of a hole of sorrow, it was endless rivers of joyful memories ... with lots of regretful rapids. At least ... Nope. All of that ... What you left behind helped me realize how great an experience it's been with you both.

"An hour ago I thought it was terrible that I was being taken from you, not the other way. For once I'll admit, love washes all your dirty past right down the drain. Makes you look into the pond and see what's really why you're alive, not just a reflection you endlessly try to rearrange to fit your ego.

"So when you and Lois forced me to stop thinking I was *Emperor of the Universe and Surrounding Areas* and throw my heart open to both of you with no reservations, no limits, ... I was really lucky ... Maybe that's a bad choice. Maybe I earned you both. I hope so. I can't put this into words but I do know right down into my bones that you both understood ... Even when I was totally ignorant."

Then it all got too hurtful. The entire sky screamed for him to just shut up. And he did.